The International Sports Academy

Soccerland

International Sports Academy

ccerland

by **Beth Choat**

MARSHALL CAVENDISH

Web site: www.marshallcavendish.us/kids

This book is a work of fiction. Names, characters, places, and incidents are products of the author's imagination and are used fictitiously. Any resemblance to actual events or locales or persons, living or dead, is entirely coincidental.

Other Marshall Cavendish Offices:
Marshall Cavendish International (Asia) Private Limited, 1 New Industrial Road, Singapore 536196 • Marshall Cavendish International (Thailand) Co Ltd. 253 Asoke, 12th Flr, Sukhumvit 21 Road, Klongtoey Nua, Wattana, Bangkok 10110, Thailand • Marshall Cavendish (Malaysia) Sdn Bhd, Times Subang, Lot 46, Subang Hi-Tech Industrial Park, Batu Tiga, 40000 Shah Alam, Selangor Darul Ehsan, Malaysia

Marshall Cavendish is a trademark of Times Publishing Limited

Library of Congress Cataloging-in-Publication Data
Choat, Beth.
Soccerland / by Beth Choat.
p. cm.—(The International Sports Academy)
Summary: Two years after her mother's death of cancer, fourteen-year-old Flora leaves the family's Maine farm for Colorado's International Sports Academy, where fierce competition could end their dream of Flora playing for U.S. Soccer.
ISBN 978-0-7614-5724-4
[1. Soccer—Fiction. 2. Competition (Psychology)—Fiction. 3. Teamwork (Sports)—Fiction. 4. Self-confidence—Fiction. 5. Family life—Maine—Fiction. 6. Maine—Fiction.] I. Title.
PZ7.C4459Soc 2010   [Fic]—dc22   2010001802

Book design by Vera Soki
Editor: Marilyn Brigham

Printed in China (E)
10 9 8 7 6 5 4 3 2

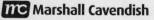 Marshall Cavendish

For DJ and GM

Contents

Chapter 1
Aroostook

"Acadia! Acadia!"

The whole school had turned out for the pep rally. The band blasted the Notre Dame fight song, the cheerleaders shook their pom-poms, and my teammates and I stood at the center of it all, on the tiny stage in the gymnasium.

Mrs. Cyr, our principal at Acadia Central School, wrapped her hands around the microphone and said, "Who's number one?"

Everyone jumped to their feet and yelled, "Acadia! Acadia!"

I looked out at the crowd of two hundred kids and teachers dressed in green and white. In less than an hour we were going to face our archenemy, Aroostook Central, for the first time since losing to them in the semifinals of last year's state soccer tournament in Bangor. We'd waited nearly twelve months for this game.

They were going down. I knew it. Everybody in the gym knew it.

Mrs. Cyr threw her arms in the air and danced along to the music with the cheerleaders. When the song ended, the crowd settled back down and Mrs. Cyr turned to the fifteen of us, standing shoulder to shoulder in our green and white uniforms. "Aroostook may be the reigning Maine State girls' soccer champions," she said. "But they aren't going to beat us this afternoon!"

Everyone cheered and the band played a few more bars of the fight song.

Mrs. Cyr smiled as she waited for the crowd to quiet down. Then she said, "Girls, we couldn't be more proud of you. You're 6 and 0—"

"So's Aroostook!" Robert Landry shouted from the top row of the bleachers.

Mrs. Cyr motioned for that jerk to zip it. "Thank you for playing devil's advocate, Robert," she said in a tone that meant, *One more word out of you and you'll be in detention. Again.* "As Robert has so diplomatically pointed out, both Acadia and Aroostook are undefeated. Aroostook's the reigning state champion, but"—Mrs. Cyr paused and let her eyes scan over the crowd—"We've got something they don't—"

Coach Roy leaned in toward the mic and yelled, "Flora Dupre!" And everyone went nuts again. My cousin Rémi yanked a school banner off the wall and ran around the gym. A bunch of younger kids took off after him.

While Mrs. Cyr rattled on about me—*Maine State Soccer Player of the Year—as a seventh grader, no less! And MVP of last year's state tournament*—I stared at my feet and tried not to look too uncomfortable. The thing was, I was proud to be from Acadia and to play for Acadia Central. I loved that we made a big deal out of high school sports in my town. Besides potato farming, school events—especially sports—were the center of our universe. Acadia was small, so everyone from kindergarteners to twelfth graders went to the same school. And the best part about being from a small school was that the state athletic association let you play high school sports once you were in the seventh grade. So lucky me, this was my second year on the girls' soccer team.

When Catherine, our captain, got up to say a few words, I had trouble paying attention. My mind was on Aroostook. It seemed like, well, an entire *year* I'd been daydreaming about this rematch. Most nights I'd fallen asleep running game scenarios through my head. How we'd capitalize on Aroostook's mistakes. How we'd score. How we'd win. How we'd *feel* when we won. And now, with kickoff just minutes away, I couldn't wait for the game to begin.

As Mrs. Cyr started to wrap up the pep rally, I caught myself lightly bouncing on the balls of my feet. This set off a chain reaction among my teammates. Suddenly we were all dancing in place, gently shaking out the muscles in our arms and legs. We were ready to play. And before we knew it, the pep rally was over and the gymnasium was emptying out. I jumped off the stage, bent down, tightened the laces on my soccer shoes one last time, and then wove my way through the crowded hallway toward the back doors.

"Go get 'em, Flora," Mrs. Vanderlip, my English teacher, said as I jogged past. I wanted to give her a big smile and yell, *Thanks, Mrs. V.,* but I needed to keep my game face on, so I dipped my head toward her quickly and kept moving through the crowd.

I pushed the back doors open. It was weird to have a game scheduled for noon. Usually we played at four o'clock, but today we had a half day of school, not on account of the game, but because it was the beginning of Harvest Break. Every year for three weeks in late September and early October all the schools in our county in northern Maine close so us kids can help get the potato crop in before winter comes. My grand-parents own a potato farm, so after today's game I was going to be picking potatoes all day, every day. That meant no school, no weekends off, and no soccer for three straight weeks.

When I got out onto the field, though, something didn't feel right. Not with my body. No, my legs were ready to go. It was just, just . . .

My teammate Rosemary tapped me on the shoulder. "Doesn't soccer typically involve two teams?"

I spun around toward the visitor's bench. It was empty. I looked to the parking lot: no Aroostook yellow bus. "What the—"

"Thought so," Rosemary said and jogged over to Cathe-rine.

Out of the corner of my eye, I saw one of the refs yank his whistle up over his head, shove it in his pocket, and then say something to Coach Roy. I watched as Coach kicked over a bench. Aroostook's bench. I ran to him. "Coach?"

"They're not coming."

"What—"

"Aroostook needed their girls in the fields, on account of the cold front coming in tonight," he said.

"What?" I said. "Like a two-hour game is going to make a difference to the harvest." I kicked Aroostook's bench. We watched it slowly try to right itself before gravity won and dumped it into a muddy puddle. "You're kidding me, right?"

Coach stepped up onto the bench with one foot, then the other. "Do I look like I'm kidding?" he said and jumped ever so slightly, his body weight causing the bench to sink deeper into the mud.

"No, but—"

"Go home," Coach said and moved toward the scorer's table.

"But—"

He glared at me. "Flora!"

Before I could turn and walk away, Rosemary jumped on my back. "Suckers," she said. "Aroostook's too afraid to play us."

I tried to shake Rosemary off, but she wouldn't let go. "Ro—"

Catherine pulled off her goalkeeper's gloves. "Easiest win in Acadia history," she said and buried them in her bag. "Now we're 7 and 0 and Aroostook's no longer undefeated."

"That's not the point," I mumbled. "We wanted to beat them fair and square."

"A win's a win," Rosemary said and slid off my back. She whispered something to Catherine, and they both looked at me. "So, Flora," Rosemary said. "Do you think your grand-father still needs us to pick potatoes this afternoon?" I looked from Rosemary to Catherine. I opened my mouth, but nothing came out. Rosemary continued, "With the game cancelled and all, we should hang out at my house for a while."

Catherine reached for Rosemary's ponytail and started to braid it. "Yeah," she said. "Then we can practice our hair for Harvest Ball."

Practice our hair? Were they insane? This was Aroostook. *Aroostook.* For one year all we'd talked about was how we were going to beat those smirky pains in the butt. How we couldn't wait to play them again, make them stop wearing those annoying blue State Champion jackets, and take down those god-awful signs on either end of their town. WELCOME TO AROOSTOOK. HOME OF THE MAINE STATE GIRLS' SOCCER CHAMPIONS.

My friends gathered up their bags and started to walk away. I felt as if I were in a dream and couldn't wake up. Then Rosemary looked over her shoulder. "Come by my place on your way home," she said. "I promise it'll be wicked fun."

"Yeah," Catherine said. "More fun than picking potatoes." And they both laughed.

I tried to speak, to shake my head no, but my body wouldn't respond.

Catherine turned around, stared briefly, and then ran toward me smiling, her gym bag slapping against her hip. I knew it! They were just pretending not to be upset. These were my friends—my *best* friends. Of course they were joking.

Catherine looked me in the eyes, hugged me quickly, and said, "See ya! Wouldn't wanna be ya."

"What?" I said, but they were already gone, giggling as they ran away. Everyone else was leaving, too, climbing into cars and school buses and pulling out of the parking lot. I wanted to yell, *No! Stop! Come back!* But everyone was disappearing so fast there was nothing I could do.

One of the refs walked up from behind and said, "Tough break, Flora." I watched him sling his bag over his shoulder and head for his pickup truck. He called out, "See ya after Harvest Break."

I took off at a full sprint, running across the soccer field, through the playground, past the big white announcement board that read GIRLS' SOCCER, ACADIA VS AROOSTOOK, 12 NOON.

When I reached the main road, I ran down the middle, my feet slapping both sides of the double yellow line. My lungs felt like they were going to explode. I ran harder. *Explode*, I thought. *See if I care.* And then my cleats slipped on an oily patch of pavement, and I landed on my butt. I didn't have the energy or the desire to pick myself up, so I lay back and sprawled out on the warm pavement. My chest heaved as I tried to catch my breath and cry at the same time. Today wasn't supposed to happen like this. This was Aroostook. *Aroostook.* We'd been looking forward to this game—at least *I* had—for almost a year.

A horn honked, and I sat bolt upright. Robert Landry stared down from the driver's side window of his dad's pickup truck. "Poor little Flora, crying for her mommy. Wah."

He floored the engine and left me in a disgusting cloud of blue exhaust.

"Idiot!" I yelled.

I lay back down on the pavement and closed my eyes. "Just run me over," I said to no one, and realized I meant it. "Put me out of my misery," I whispered. I looked up at the blue sky and imagined the headline in tomorrow's newspaper: SOCCER STAR DUPRE CRUSHED.

I lifted my head, looked up Main Street. No cars coming. I looked down Main Street. Nothing. "Crushed," I said and stood up.

I'd left my backpack at the field, but I didn't care. No way was I going back to school. I headed home. In a daze.

Chapter 2
Harvest Break

A half hour later I reached the cut-off road to our farm. I'd stopped crying by then, but I was still totally crushed. When I looked up and saw the black-and-white DEAD END sign at the head of our road, I took off my soccer shoes and hurled them at the sign. The metal twanged so hard I could feel it in my chest. It felt good. I scrambled into the ditch and picked up my shoes. "Aroostook?" I said and threw one. *Twang!* "Had to stay home and pick?" I threw the other. *Twang!* "Stupid. Potatoes." I grabbed my shoes back up off the ground. Cocked my arm. "Couldn't wait a couple of hours?" *Twang!* "For the game to be over?" *Twang!*

I walked up close to the sign. I'd added a few good dents to go along with the bullet holes some idiot, probably Robert Landry or one of his genius older brothers, had already put in it. I looked down at my socks. They used to be white. *Who cares.* I picked up my soccer shoes and headed home.

When I crested the final hill before the farm, I looked down into the valley and saw a couple of dozen people: my cousins, aunts, uncles, and a few neighbors, kneeling in the dark furrows handpicking potatoes. They were laughing and chatting among themselves. How could they be so happy? Didn't they know what just happened?

I watched my cousin Rémi run up the hill toward me. Rémi was the closest thing I had to a brother—our dads were brothers, so basically we'd been raised like twins—but like most brothers, Rémi didn't *get* me. Soccer wasn't his thing. He was all about family and the farm. Acadia was his world—always had been, always would be. He tolerated my soccer dream as just that, a dream, fantasy. Sure, he was proud of me, but Rémi didn't see the big soccer picture—college scholarship, national teams, the Olympics and World Cup.

"Hey," Rémi said, all out of breath. "Sorry about the game." I felt a tear run down my left cheek. I squeezed my eyes shut. "Flora?"

I raised my hand. "Don't." A second tear rolled down my cheek. I wiped it away. "I hate Harvest Break!" I screamed.

"You don't mean that," Rémi said and stopped walking. He expected me to stop, too, but I didn't. Instead I ran down the hill and didn't look back.

"Flora!"

I kept my head down as I ran through the long grass at the edge of the old paddock toward the farmhouse. I wasn't mad at Rémi, or my family or even about Harvest Break. It was just that I'd wanted to play Aroostook so badly it hurt. Physically. But mostly, I was tired, tired of living on the edge of the world—the soccer world, anyway.

"Flora!"

I turned around and yelled, "Rémi, shut up!"

It was unfair to scream at Rémi, but I knew soon enough

he'd get over it, I'd cool down, and everything would go back to normal. Just like real siblings, Rémi and I either got along great or we were at each other's throats.

Rémi was right about one thing, though: I didn't hate Harvest Break. Normally, I liked it—loved it—but this year everything got off on the wrong foot. Harvest Break was supposed to start with me, well, Acadia destroying Aroostook, and then my uncles and I would spend three weeks in the fields rehashing the game while picking potatoes. But with the game not happening, I was looking at spending three frustrating weeks crawling around on my hands and knees in the dirt.

In August, Coach Roy and I had talked about how this could be my breakthrough year—my chance to make the jump from high school soccer to a girls' national team. I enjoyed playing for Acadia, but after days like today, I knew I needed more. My dream was to play for the U.S.A., and at fourteen, I was old enough—and according to Coach Roy, good enough—to try out for the Under-15s, the youngest U.S. Soccer Girls' National Team. All summer Coach wrote e-mails and made phone calls to U.S. Soccer to try and get me an invite to one of their Under-14 Girls' National Team Identification Camps, which are for girls ages fourteen and under. Coach said if I could get in front of the national coaches at an Identification Camp, I'd have a good chance of making the Under-15 Girls' National Team. I hoped Coach was right, but it was September and I still didn't have an invite.

I climbed the little hill to the farmhouse and went in through the back. In the mudroom, I pulled off my socks and flung them on top of the washing machine. I heard Mémère, my grandmother, singing to herself in the kitchen. I quietly scooted down the hallway and up the back staircase to my bedroom.

"Flora?" Nothing got by Mémère. "That you?"

"Ayuh," I said when I got to my bedroom upstairs.

"I heard about the game."

"You mean, about those buttheads from Aroostook," I said, collapsing onto my bed.

"Language, young lady." I listened as Mémère opened and closed drawers in the kitchen. "There'll be other soccer games, my dear," she said.

"It's not fair." I buried my head under my pillow.

A few minutes later, Mémère appeared in my bedroom doorway. "No, I guess it's not fair," she said. "Soccer's important, but it's not the most important thing today. With this cold snap, we need you kids to help us get the potatoes in quickly." She handed me a cup of hot apple cider. "Don't want to see anyone lose their farm."

I raised the mug to my lips and pretended to sip from it. I wanted to say, *All the farms around here are going under. Are a few extra barrels of potatoes really going to be the difference between people keeping their farms and losing them?*

But I knew I couldn't say that. So I just nodded, like I agreed with my grandmother.

"You're a good girl, Flora Dupre."

I nodded again, but this time I felt guilty. *Actually, I'm a selfish girl. I don't care about potatoes. Sell the farm, don't sell the farm. I just want to play soccer.* I looked into my mug, took a big sip of cider, and felt it burn as it went down my throat. I let out a gasp.

"Careful," Mémère said as she walked out of the room.

☸   ☸   ☸

I lay back on my bed and let my tears soak into the pillow. I knew what people said about me, that I was the best soccer player—boy or girl—ever to come out of Maine. But I wasn't an idiot. Maine wasn't a soccer hotbed. If I lived in New Jersey or California and people said the same things, I wouldn't have to beg U.S. Soccer for a U-14 Girls' National Team ID Camp invite or worry about getting a college scholarship. But living in the sticks of northern Maine, it was hard to get anyone outside this frozen state to pay attention. I wished someone could wave a wand and magically transport me from Acadia Central to a spot on a U.S. Girls' National Team and a college soccer scholarship.

"Flora?" Rémi called from the kitchen, where he was talking with Mémère.

"Ayuh."

"You coming?" he asked.

"Just changing my clothes," I said. "Be right there." But I didn't move from my bed.

Chapter 3
Soccerland

A few minutes later I heard the back screen door slap shut. There was no noise from the kitchen, so I figured Mémère must have gone with Rémi to the fields.

I got up quietly from the bed and tiptoed across the hall into my father's bedroom. I opened his closet door, and reached up on the top shelf, stretching my arm as far as possible. Had someone moved the box? I jumped up, but the light was burned out, so I couldn't see a thing. I reached again, this time deep onto the back of the shelf, and hooked my fingertips on the edge of the box, gently guiding it toward me until I was able to lower it down with both hands.

I set the old wooden box on the floor, sat down next to it, and removed the lid. Ma's scarf was still on top. I lifted the silky blue material to my face, closed my eyes, and inhaled. It had been two years since Ma died, but I could still smell her. I tied the scarf around my head, just like Ma did when the chemotherapy took her hair, her beautiful blonde hair.

I reached into the box and looked at the first photo my

fingers touched. Ma and me at County General. Laughing in her hospital bed. I tried to remember what Pa had said to make us laugh so hard but couldn't. I laid the photo on the floor and reached for another. Me in my crib, hugging a soccer ball. I loved that one. Where was the one of me licking the soccer ball? I fished through the stack, found it. I laughed at my pudgy little self. Licking a soccer ball. What was up with that?

I dug deeper into the box and pulled a bunch of photos out from underneath. Oh, Ma in her Acadia Central uniform. I ran my fingers over Ma's face. Everyone said I looked like her. I didn't see it. I turned the photo a little to the side and squinted at my reflection in the mirror on the closet door. Maybe it was the hair, or maybe it was because we both loved soccer.

Ma was about my age when she fell in love with soccer. She loved everything about it, was voted Most Valuable Player four years in a row at Acadia Central. She wanted to play in college, but when she graduated high school she married Pa and moved into the farmhouse, with Mémère and Pépère. Seven months later I was born. Ma told me she wanted me to be a soccer player from the day she knew I was in her belly.

I moved a bunch of things around in the box until I found a pale pink hospital bracelet. I smiled. Ma hated pink. This must have been the last bracelet she wore. The letters hadn't faded. *Evangeline L. Dupre. Female.* Duh. *30 years old.*

When Ma started to get sick, she came up with a fantasyland she called Soccerland. It was where she went, where we both went, to get away from the cancer.

I hated County General Hospital, hated seeing Ma sick, but I always tried to be there when she had chemotherapy. She usually had it around three o'clock, so I'd rush over after school and keep her company until Pa got out of the fields. I'd run into her hospital room, throw my backpack and jacket in the corner, help Ma recline in the big leather chair, and we'd talk about soccer, all the while trying to ignore the nurses and the needles and the beeping machines.

One day near the end of Ma's life—which I didn't know was the end, but Ma must have known—I came into the room and found a nurse hunched over Ma. I peeked around the nurse, didn't see Ma's chest moving, and panicked. "Is she—"

The nurse shook her head and whispered, "Sleeping." The nurse wiped Ma's arm with a little pad of alcohol and inserted an IV needle into her vein. Then she looked up at me and said, "It's okay. Talk to your Ma."

But before I could say anything, Ma opened her eyes. "Flora," she said. "Let's go to Soccerland."

I kissed Ma's forehead and gently lowered myself onto the arm of her chair. "1999 World Cup Finals?" I asked.

"Ayuh," Ma said.

"Okay, then. China versus the U.S. at the Rose Bowl."

"Stinkin' hot Los Angeles day," Ma said.

"Ninety thousand fans." I watched the nurse tape the IV to the bruised crook of Ma's left arm. Ma scrunched up her face. I forced myself—us—out of County General and into Soccerland. "Nearly two hours of double-overtime soccer without a goal."

Ma closed her eyes and exhaled slowly. "Penalty kick shootout."

I could tell she was tired. "I'll jump ahead to the good stuff, okay?" Ma nodded. "After four shots the score's tied at 2–2. It's China's turn. Their girl fires a shot close to the middle of the net, but it gets knocked wide."

"Good old Briana Scurry in goal," Ma said.

"Ayuh, then Kristine Lilly steps up. Bangs it past China's keeper. The place goes nuts. 3–2 U.S." Ma shifted in her chair.

"You okay?" I asked.

"My stomach's a little upset," she said. "Keep going."

"You know this part. China comes back, scores. It's 3–3. But then,"—I gently drummed my fingers on the back of Ma's chair—"it's Mia Hamm's turn."

Ma turned her head ever so slightly, like it weighed a thousand pounds, and peeked at me through half-open eyes. "Remember how scared Mia looked? She hated that kind of pressure, didn't she?"

"Yeah, but—"

"She scored," Ma said.

"Put the U.S. up 4–3." Ma covered her mouth, like she was going to be sick. "Ma?"

"Hand me the bedpan." Ma took the pan from me and rested it on her stomach.

I glanced up at the half empty IV bag hanging from the pole above Ma's chair, closed my eyes, and forced myself, both of us, to stay in Soccerland. "The place goes crazy," I said.

"We did, too." Ma laughed. "Remember? Pa came running in from the barn. 'What the Sam Hill's going on in here?' You were jumping up and down on the couch, yelling 'Mia! Mia!' at the top of your lungs."

Ma laughed at the memory. I did, too, even though I didn't remember that day. How could I? I was three years old. My memories of that game were from watching the video, looking at the magazines Ma had saved, and because that game was pretty much Ma's all-time favorite sports moment. Of course, I never told her I didn't remember watching the game live on

TV. She wouldn't have believed me anyway.

"China scores again," I said. "It's 4–4. This is it. Just one more penalty shot, and the game's over."

"Can't let China win," Ma said.

"Can't," I said. "Brandi Chastain steps up—"

"We were two inches away from the TV," Ma said. "And Pa was yelling at us to get out of the way."

"So the U.S. team links arms and forms a line a few yards behind Brandi," I said. "And Brandi, cool as a cucumber, doesn't even look up at China's keeper. She drills it—"

"Left-footed—"

"Ayuh, buries the ball just inside the right post."

"She can't believe it," Ma said. "The U.S. has won the World Cup."

"Brandi drops to her knees, rips off her jersey, and swings it overhead—"

Ma laughed. "I'll never forget the look on your face. Brandi Chastain's celebrating on national TV in her black running bra, and you're screaming, 'Ma, she's almost nekk-ed! Nekk-ed!'"

"It's not funny." Ma opened one eye, stifled a laugh. "I was three years old," I said.

Ma pretended to nudge me off the chair. "The U.S. Women win the World Cup, the greatest victory in the history of U.S. Women's soccer, and all you can think about is her bra. 'Her bra, Ma! Her bra. Everyone can see her bra!'"

"Okay," I said. "It's a little bit funny." Ma cocked an eyebrow at me. "It's a lot funny."

Ma lightly stroked my thigh with her fingertips. After a few minutes, her hand slid off my leg, and her breathing slowed. I thought she'd fallen asleep, but then she said, "Imagine what it must have been like to be on that team. On that field."

"Ma," I said, "one day I'm going to play for the U.S. Women's National Team."

"Yes, you are, and don't let anyone in Acadia tell you you're not." Ma handed me the empty bedpan. I placed it on the floor, tucked the blanket up around her neck, and she closed her eyes. "Follow your dream," she said. "No matter what."

"Soccerland," I heard myself say, and I was back in the closet.

"Flora?" Mémère had returned from the fields and was on her way upstairs.

"Coming." I shoved everything back into the box, slapped the cover on, and hoisted it onto the top shelf of Pa's closet. I ran into the hallway and nearly cleaned Mémère out as I rounded the corner at the top of the stairs.

"They need you in the fields," she said.

"On my way." I squeezed past her.

I felt Ma's scarf slide off the back of my head. "I'll take that," Mémère said gathering the scarf in her hands.

I didn't look back. And Mémère didn't say anything else. Because no one talked about Ma anymore. It was like she never existed. For them.

But she did for me. Every minute of every day.

No matter what.

Chapter 4
Potatoland

"There she is," one of my aunts called out, and everyone looked up from their crouched positions in the field.

"Our almost heroine."

"MVP of the game that never happened."

"Flora Dupre. Soccer Goddess."

I grabbed an empty basket from the edge of the field. "We would have won," I said.

"Heck, yeah," Uncle Henri, Pa's oldest brother, yelled.

"Flora?" Rémi held up a rotten potato. Clearly, all was forgiven. I nodded yes, and he gently lobbed the potato toward me. I side-volleyed it toward the edge of the field, but it came off my laces funny and rocketed toward Rémi's dad, two rows to our right. "Heads up!" we shouted.

"What—" The potato flew past Uncle Al's head.

"Her bad," Rémi said to his dad and then tackled me into the damp, dark soil. I flipped him over and pinned him to the ground. "For the record," I said as loudly as possible, "those ninnies from Aroostook would have been crying like babies when we were done with them."

The farm, whether I liked it or not, was the center of the Dupre universe. My relatives had worked this land for more than two hundred years, ever since my great, great, great whatevers moved here from just over the border in Canada. Even today we thought of ourselves as Franco American, rather than just American, and we spoke a French dialect called Valley French. We still harvested potatoes the old-fashioned way—by hand. We used a machine called a digger to help yank the potatoes out of the ground, but after that we collected everything by hand. One potato at a time.

All of our neighbors used a machine called a harvester to suck up the potatoes like a giant vacuum cleaner, but my grandfather, Pépère, refused to move into the twenty-first century. That's why all my relatives and lots of our friends helped out during Harvest Break. Picking potatoes by hand was a lot harder than sucking them up with a harvester, but it was also a lot more fun. We liked working side by side as a family during Harvest Break, with a common goal, to bring in the crop. The thing is, us Dupres, we didn't know any differently.

That afternoon, I listened to my relatives chatter away in a combination of French and English. Before I dropped to my knees and got to work, I tucked my hair out of the way and pulled the hood of my sweatshirt up. I placed my basket on the ground next to me and started to load potatoes into it, one by one.

At one point I stopped, reached up under my hoodie, and touched my hair, trying to remember what Ma's scarf had felt like. I missed her. I missed her so much. The way she ran her fingers through my hair, the way she smelled, like butter cake batter before you put it in the oven. Sometimes in the early morning, I could almost hear her padding around the kitchen.

I kept a framed photo of Ma under my mattress. At night, I liked to slide it out from under the mattress and talk to her. It seemed every single day for the last two years, there was something I wanted to tell her, something I ended up keeping to myself.

Mostly I worried about getting out of Acadia. As much as I loved it, I didn't want to stay on the farm. I needed to play soccer for the U.S., and to get a college scholarship to some-place like the University of North Carolina, where I could play soccer year-round. With Ma gone, the only person I could talk to was Coach Roy. Pa thought I should be a gym teacher and my friends, like Rémi, didn't get it. Like today, how Rosemary and Catherine seemed *excited* when Aroostook cancelled. Whenever I talked about being a professional soccer player, my friends would laugh and say things like, "Whatever, Le-Bron James." I had learned that it was easier to sit back and take it, but what I wanted to say was, *What about Mia Hamm, Venus, Serena, Michelle Wie, the girls in the WNBA? They get paid a lot of money to play sports.* But I kept my mouth shut. It wasn't worth it. Kids in Acadia couldn't imagine being a pro athlete. But I wasn't like them. I knew I could be a pro soccer player; all I needed was a chance. A chance to get out of Aca-dia and be seen by U.S. National Team coaches.

I leaned back and looked up at the sky. "One chance," I said to no one.

I picked up my basket, walked to the end of my section, and dumped it into one of the sturdy cedar barrels. The pota-toes thundered into the barrel and drowned out the chatter of the pickers around me. In the distance I saw Rémi, hunched over in his Red Sox jacket, picking away. I walked the length of the row to reach him and collapsed into the churned earth next to him.

"How's it going?" he said.

He seemed to have forgiven me for earlier, so I didn't say anything. "My knees are already killing me, and we've got three more weeks of this," I said.

"We'll survive."

"Ayuh. Harvest Break's harder than going to school."

We looked toward the barn, where Pa had fired up the tractor. The gears ground loud and hard. "That thing's gonna explode one day," Rémi said.

The tractor, with the digger attached, lurched toward the far end of our field. Pa looked up. When he caught my eye, he raised his chin ever so slightly. I juggled two potatoes like they were hot out of the oven. He looked away.

A gym teacher, huh? I kicked a rotten potato all the way across the field, into the woods. I heard it smack against a tree.

Ma used to say, "Those who can't play, coach." Well, I could play. I *would* play. For a national team.

Chapter 5
First Step

We picked until the sun dropped behind the trees and we could barely see our white gloves against the soil. When the floodlight outside the barn flickered on, everyone started to head in.

Everyone except me.

"Drop those any harder into the basket and you'll spoil them." It was Pépère.

"Sorry," I said to my grandfather. "I was just thinking about something."

"Like the Aroostook game?" I nodded and shifted from my knees to my butt. The cold, damp earth seeped through my jeans. "This time of year, potatoes come first," he said. "I wish they didn't, for you young ones, but they do."

I tried to wipe the dirt off the knees of my jeans. They were stained and wet from the damp soil. Pépère motioned toward the barn. "You've got a visitor."

"Who?"

"Coach Roy." Pépère offered me his hand. "Says he's got

something important to tell you." He pulled me up off the ground. "Let's go see what that coach of yours has up his sleeve," he said, tugging my hoodie down over my eyes.

Coach Roy sat swinging his legs from the tailgate of his pickup truck. He dangled my backpack in the air. "This belong to anyone around here?" I quickly snatched it away.

"What's that?" Pépère asked.

"Nothing," Coach Roy and I said together.

Coach Roy changed the subject. "So, Mr. Dupre, how's the picking coming along? This girl doing her share?"

"When she's not kicking 'em into the woods."

"Flora—" Coach looked at me and tried not to laugh.

"I only do it to the rotten ones. Ask Rémi."

Pépère turned to Coach Roy and said, "Sorry to hear about the game this afternoon."

"Thanks, but you haven't heard the worst of it," Coach Roy said. "Aroostook didn't show up, and now they're upset the refs recorded it as a loss."

"They didn't even tell you until the last minute they weren't coming," I said, but both men ignored me.

"So what's gonna happen?" Pépère asked.

"The rules are pretty clear. You don't show up, you forfeit. It's a loss." Coach exhaled, and the cold air turned his breath into a big, puffy white cloud. "But Aroostook doesn't want to ruin their perfect season. They want to reschedule the game."

Reschedule? Fine by me. Then we can beat 'em fair and square.

Coach waved his hands in front of his face like he was batting away a pesky black fly. "Enough about Aroostook."

The men continued to make small talk about the farm while I tried to figure out why Coach had stopped by. I didn't need my backpack for the next three weeks, so I knew it wasn't about that. Maybe Coach had heard back from U.S. Soccer about a U-14 Girls' National Team ID Camp invitation.

Don't go there, I told myself. I didn't want to get excited for nothing.

"You know what, Coach?" I heard Pépère say. "I do believe our Flora is taller than you."

I knew I'd grown over the summer—all my pants were too short—but could I really be taller than Coach Roy? Pépère walked to the edge of the woods. "Okay, you two, let me get a measuring stick." Pépère poked around in the underbrush until he found a small tree branch about three feet long.

"Let's go, back-to-back, eyes straight ahead," Pépère said as Coach and I leaned against each other and rose up on our toes to gain an extra inch or two. But Pépère wanted no part of that. "Heels on the ground."

"Aw, Mr. Dupre," Coach said. "That twig isn't even straight."

"Are you criticizing my magic measuring stick?"

"No sir, I sure am not."

Pépère balanced the stick on our heads. After several seconds of hemming and hawing, he said, "She's got you by half an inch, Coach."

"Yes. Yes. Yes." I threw my arms in the air and danced around like I'd won the World Cup.

Coach Roy shook his head and smiled. "Fourteen years old and five feet nine inches. My goodness, wait till those U.S. National Team coaches see you."

See me? Was I going to get a tryout with U.S. Soccer? *Don't, Flora.*

We all laughed. Pépère invited Coach to join us for dinner and then headed toward the barn. I opened the cab of Coach's pickup, grabbed a soccer ball I'd noticed sitting on the seat, dropped it onto the dirt driveway, and backheeled it to him.

We passed the ball between us. Back in his day, Coach Roy led Acadia to the boys' state title in his senior year and then played on a scholarship at Long Island University in New York. The summer Ma died, Coach moved back to Acadia to work at the school and coach soccer. He wanted to coach the boys' team, but the only opening was for the girls' team. Lucky us. Two years down the road, and all the boys were jealous.

We continued to pass the ball in silence. I knew something big was up because Coach was taking so long to tell me. Finally he spoke. "Remember that Olympic Development Program tryout I took you to in Boston last month?"

Remember? I was still replaying the conversation I'd had with Kristine Lilly. *The* Kristine Lilly, star of the U.S. Women's National Team, who said I reminded her of Abby Wambach. *Yes, I remember.* But I decided to play it cool. "Ayuh," I said as I rolled the ball up the back of my left heel, flicked it in the air with my right foot, and then kicked it up and over my shoulder with my left heel.

"Sweet rainbow," Coach said as he briefly trapped the ball on his chest and then dropped it onto the top of his right foot. "Here's the thing," he said continuing to balance the ball on his foot. "The Region 1 U.S. Soccer coaches in Boston were very impressed with you."

"Yeah, I know. They named me to the Boston-area ODP team—"

Coach volleyed me the ball. "We both know you can't play for a Boston team living seven hours away in Acadia. But chin up, it gets better." I trapped the ball under my left foot. "You know I've been writing e-mails and making phone calls all summer, but what you don't know is that the Boston ODP coaches submitted your name to U.S. Soccer for the U-14 National Development Program."

I felt like I was going to pass out. "The coaches in Boston think I'm good enough to play for a national team?"

Coach leaned against the pickup. He motioned for me to hop up on the tailgate. "We all agree that with some extra coaching and more opportunities to play, you could be on a national team. Kristine Lilly personally called the head of the U-14 National Development Program and said they had to bring you in for a tryout."

Was he really saying what I thought he was?

"I know it's Harvest Break." Coach fiddled with the strings on his hoodie. "But I just heard from U.S. Soccer, and they're holding a two-week Under-14 Girls' National Team Identification Camp, for the best thirteen- and fourteen-year-olds in the country, starting on Monday. They want you there."

I felt dizzy. "C-c-can I go?"

"We'll have to see what your family says. It's an incredible opportunity. ID Camp's the first step toward making a national team."

"Like the Under-15s?"

"And the Under-16s, maybe even the Under-17s. You know they're gonna play in the FIFA U-17 Women's World Cup," Coach said. "But let's not get ahead of ourselves."

"So this means . . ."

"You're on your way to one day playing soccer for the United States of America."

I jumped off the truck, ran toward the ball we'd left in the dirt, and kicked it up and over Coach's pickup and into the backyard of the farmhouse. I ripped off my UNC sweatshirt, yelled "Goooooooooooooooaaaaaaaaaaallllllllll!" at the top of my lungs, and raced around the pitch-black farmyard.

Chapter 6
Coach v. Pa

Mémère was busy at the stove when we entered the warm kitchen. "Mrs. Dupre," Coach said. "It smells delicious in here."

"Well, Coach, we sure are pleased you've decided to join us for dinner." Mémère shuffled across the kitchen floor to give him a hug. "Pull up a chair. I'm sorry we don't have any booster seats left; you'll have to sit in a big-boy chair, is that okay?"

"Big-boy chair?" Coach said.

Mémère howled with laughter. "You know, since you'll be the shortest one at the table." Mémère looked at me. "Taller than your coach, huh?"

Coach laughed. "Let me guess. I'm so small you're going to serve shrimp for dinner?"

"I wouldn't dare do that to you, Shorty—I mean, Coach. I don't want you to feel self-conscious around us towering Dupres."

I helped set the table and before long, the five of us—Mémère and Pépère, Pa, Coach Roy, and I—were settled around the old kitchen table.

After we'd passed the food, Pépère said, "So Coach, what's this news you have?"

Coach Roy and I smiled at each other. "U.S. Soccer has invited Flora to a national team tryout."

I held my breath. Everyone stopped eating, except Pa. It was like he hadn't heard what Coach said. Pa lifted his glass of milk and drained it. When he reached for the milk container I wanted to throw a dinner roll at him.

"A tryout?" Pépère said. "Joseph, what do you think of that?"

Pa looked up. "Sorry. What'd you say?"

Coach tried again; this time he spoke directly to Pa. "When I took Flora down to Boston this summer, the regional coaches were very impressed. They believe, with some guidance and more playing time, she can eventually play for the U.S. Women's National Team."

I wanted to add, *In the Olympics and the World Cup.* Instead, I looked around the table and willed my family to understand just how important this was.

Mémère clucked her tongue, which meant, *Go on. I'm listening.* No one else said anything. I drew in a deep breath and held it. I was afraid to move a muscle and jinx the whole thing.

"One of the first steps for a young girl to make the U.S. Women's National Team is to be invited to an Under-14 Girls' National Team Identification Camp," Coach said. "The one Flora's been invited to is in Colorado. For two weeks, national team coaches will evaluate her skills and potential through training and games. There's talk that at the end of the camp they might name some of the girls to the U.S. Under-15 Girls' National Team."

"Colorado?" Pépère said. "When would she go?"

"She'd fly out on Sunday and be back in two weeks. Since it's Harvest Break, she wouldn't miss any school." Coach looked from Pa to my grandparents. "Of course, I know it would be an enormous sacrifice to let Flora go during the harvest—"

"It's a nice idea, Coach, but you know we don't have the money to send Flora to Colorado," Pa said and started to eat again, which was his way of saying, *End of discussion*.

But Coach Roy wasn't going to give up that easily. "Oh sorry, I should have mentioned: U.S. Soccer will pay for everything," he said. "And if you'd like, I can take Flora to and from the airport. Plus, she'll live for free at the International Sports Academy."

"I will?" The grown-ups looked at me. It was like they'd forgotten I was at the table. *Should have kept my mouth shut!*

Mémère said, "All right, young lady, it's about time you wash up and get ready for bed. Let the adults talk this out."

I placed my plate in the sink and walked slowly out of the kitchen. But the moment I rounded the corner, I flew up the stairs, two at a time. In a matter of seconds I was lying on my bedroom floor, looking down and listening in on the adults. My bedroom had what I liked to think of as a secret snooping post, a metal heating vent in the floor that allowed heat to rise from the kitchen and warm my bedroom. No one knew that if I leaned over this vent I could see and hear everything that happened in the kitchen.

So that night, I propped my elbows on either side of the vent, looked down, and listened to my future unfold.

Chapter 7
Farm, Shmarm

I listened to Coach trying to explain everything as my family—well, mainly Mémère—fired off questions. Finally, Coach Roy left and the conversation between my grandparents and Pa switched from English to French. I knew to pay extra-special attention now, because in the Dupre farmhouse, all the good stuff was discussed in French.

"So, Joseph," Mémère said to Pa. "What do you think?"

I watched Pa through the metal slats of the vent. He didn't respond to his mother, just shook his head, picked up his coffee mug, and stared into it.

"Joseph?"

"I don't like it." Pa placed the mug on the table, a little too firmly. "She's too young."

"It's two weeks," Mémère said.

Pépère turned to his son. "That girl's got a good head on her shoulders. What are you worried about?"

"Fourteen's too young," Pa said. "And anyway, we need her in the fields."

Mémère clapped her hands together. "Joseph, you're be-ing unreasonable."

I slid a few inches forward so I could see all three of them. They looked like statues staring at each other. The only sound that rose up from the kitchen was the tick of the clock over the sink.

Pa shifted in his chair. "Oh, Ma, I don't know. Maybe you're right." He rested his chin in his hands and stared at the table. "I want what's best for Flora, I do." His voice was muffled. "I'm just so tired."

I should have moved away from the heating vent then, but I didn't. I couldn't. This was my future they were talking about. My life.

I watched Mémère reach out and stroke Pa's arm. "I miss her," he said.

I opened my mouth, but no sound came out. Ma! They were talking about Ma!

"We all do," Mémère said. "Especially Flora."

"I don't know how to be a parent anymore. I don't know how to do it without her—without Evangeline."

Pépère scooted his chair back from the table. The noise caused Pa to raise his head and look at his father. "*Écoutez*, Joseph," Pépère said. "If Evangeline were here right now, we know what she'd say—"

Pa slammed his hands on the table. "Well, she's not here right now. You know why? Because she's dead. And now it's just me." Pa put his fists to his eyes. After several seconds he cleared his throat. "*Je suis désolé. Pardonnez-moi.*"

I tried again to move away from the vent, but I was frozen to my bedroom floor.

Pa blew his nose into his napkin and then looked at his

parents. "I couldn't do this, I couldn't raise Flora, without you two."

"We're not going anywhere, son," Pépère said. "We'll always be here for you. And Flora."

Mémère reached over and rubbed Pa's back. "Evangeline would be so proud of our Flora. Getting invited to a U.S. Soccer team tryout. Boys-oh-boys." Mémère untied her apron and rested it in her lap. "That wife of yours is dancing in heaven right now." She leaned her head back, closed her eyes. "Listen."

Pa looked up. I flinched, afraid he could see me through the metal grate. My heart raced. I leaned back until I couldn't see him anymore.

"Evangeline loved that Flora shared her passion for soccer," Mémère said.

"Remember how, toward the end," Pa said, "all she wanted to do was talk about Soccerland with Flora?"

"Couldn't blame her," Pépère said and shook his head. "Goddamn cancer . . ."

Mémère looked at Pa. "You heard what Coach said— Flora's got a gift."

"That girl will kick anything," Pépère said. "Including my potatoes."

All three of them laughed. "We owe it to Flora," Mémère said, "and to Evangeline—"

"What about the farm?" said Pa.

"Farm, shmarm," Pépère said. "The sight of my granddaughter in a U.S.A. jersey? Why, that's worth all the potatoes in Maine."

They were silent for a moment.

"Son?" Mémère said.

"I don't know. I still think she's too young." Pa looked at his parents. "If it were up to me, I'd say no. I don't want her out of my sight, but if you two think she should go, she can go."

Silently, I rolled onto my back, raised my arms and legs, and wildly shook them in the air. Then I reached under my mattress for Ma's photo, pulled it out, and hugged it to my chest.

Forget Soccerland, Ma. I'm going to Colorado. To the ISA. To U.S. freakin' Soccer.

Chapter 8
Merci, Pa

Later that evening, when Pa knocked on my bedroom door, I was still lying on the floor. As he opened the door I remembered the photo and tried to push it under the bed.

"Don't," he said.

"But—"

"It's okay." Pa sat down on the hardwood floor. He was still wearing his muddy overalls and flannel shirt. Pa picked up the framed photo. "She was beautiful, your Ma." He smiled at me. "She loved you so much."

Tears streamed down my cheeks. We sat in silence, talking without talking.

Then, the words just tumbled out. "Why don't you talk about Ma anymore?"

"I do—"

"You don't," I said. "No one does. No one even mentions her name."

Pa stared at the floor. "You're right," he said, "we don't."

"Why?"

"Because . . ."

"Because it hurts?"

Pa nodded. "Flora, sometimes it's easier to pretend it didn't happen."

"Easier?" I said. "Easier for whom?"

"Everyone—"

"Not for me." I grabbed Ma's photo. "I talk to Ma every day. Did you know that?" He shook his head. "It's like you guys want to forget about her."

Pa's head snapped up and he looked at me. "*Mon Dieu, non.* Every day I look at you . . . and I see your mother. Your hair, your voice . . . and now your height."

I wanted to ask if this was a good or a bad thing, but I said, "I miss Ma. I'm afraid we're going to forget about her."

Pa looked at the picture again. "We're not going to let that happen. Your Ma loved us. The only thing she was worried about at the end, was us." Pa's voice got all snuffly. He pulled the cuff of his flannel sleeve up over his left palm, pressed it against one eye, then the other. "*Ma chérie*, she wanted us to be happy."

"To follow our dreams," I said.

"Ayuh, to follow our dreams. And your dream is to play soccer for the U.S.A." He picked up one of my soccer shoes, turned it over, and ran his fingers over the hard rubber studs. "Coach tells me this Identification Camp tryout is hot stuff . . . so it sounds like we've got to get you out to Colorado."

I scooted over the heating vent and threw my arms around his neck. "*Merci*, Pa!"

Pa reached into the front pocket of his overalls and took out a small pair of pliers and an antique silver charm bracelet. "Oh," I said. Ma had worn that bracelet every day. When Pa gave it to her on their wedding day, it was just a silver bracelet, but he'd promised to add a charm every year on their anniversary. And he had.

"I thought you buried it with Ma," I said.

Pa shook his head. "Been holding onto it," he said. "Figured I'd give it to you at some point. Just didn't know when." Pa ran the bracelet between his fingers. He stopped at a pair of tiny, silver baby booties. "I gave these to your Ma when you were born."

"They're so cute." I lifted them gently with my fingertip and smiled at Pa.

"So were you." He laughed to himself. "You know what Ma nicknamed you as a baby?" I shook my head. *"Pample-mousse!"*

"Grapefruit?" I said. "Seriously? Ma called me *pample-mousse*? That's cruel."

"You were a big, round ball of baby. Ma used to say, 'She's so cute I could eat her.'"

Pa slid the bracelet around again until he came to a beautiful silver soccer ball. "Speaking of round balls."

"It's perfectly detailed," I said. "You can even see the stitching."

"I gave this to Ma on our third anniversary."

"Very romantic—"

"She thought so." Pa's cheeks flushed red. "I was thinking, how about when you're in Colorado you could wear the soccer ball charm on that chain around your neck, and I'll attach the booties to my keychain."

I hadn't seen this Pa in forever. I realized that I'd missed him. I nodded and wiped my eyes with the backs of my hands, then watched as Pa pried open the delicate silver links that held the charms to the bracelet. "Careful," I said. Pa cradled the booties and soccer ball in his large palm.

I handed him the silver chain from around my neck. He slipped the soccer ball on the chain and closed the link with his pliers. "Perfect," he said. I turned around, lifted my hair, and Pa re-clasped the chain around my neck.

After he'd attached the booties to his keychain Pa stood up with Ma's photo in his hand. "What do you say we put this right here on the bureau?"

"Perfect," I whispered.

And it really was.

When he left the room, I looked at myself in the mirror, reached up, and touched the charm. Pa was right; I did look like Ma.

Chapter 9
Last Touch

It was still dark outside when I looked at the ancient clock on my nightstand. It was set to go off any minute. I slid the alarm tab to off. There was no danger I'd fall back to sleep. I'd waited my whole life—my whole soccer life—for today.

I pulled the covers tight around my neck and smiled. The house was silent, but I could smell bacon, so I knew Mémère was up. I dressed quickly, shoved my nightgown and toothbrush into my duffel bag, and zipped it shut. Coach Roy would be here soon to take me to the airport.

In the kitchen, Mémère had prepared eggs to go with the bacon, and as an extra-special treat, she'd baked my favorite banana chocolate chip muffins. It was Ma's recipe. She handed me two muffins wrapped in tinfoil. "In case you get hungry. I've heard airplane food is terrible."

I hugged Mémère and sat down at the table. As I began to eat, Pépère came in from the barn. "Our world traveler," he said. "How's it feel to be the first Dupre to fly on a plane?"

"Oh . . ." I rested my fork on my plate. I hadn't thought about the plane.

Mémère wiped her hands on her apron. "What I'd give to fly across the country on a plane."

"Ayuh," Pépère said. "And then you'd have to get off the plane and play soccer with a bunch of kids."

"I'll play soccer with you, you crazy old man," Mémère said and pretended to chase Pépère around the kitchen. Pa and Coach Roy came through the back door and joined in the chase. Before long, the kitchen was full of my cousins and aunts and uncles. Word had spread about my ID Camp tryout.

When I stepped outside, the sun had just started to rise over the fields. It felt like a true celebration. Everyone laughed and joked around. Some of my younger cousins had painted signs to wish me luck. Rémi stood next to Pépère's old red truck. It was decorated with streamers and a giant papier-mâché soccer ball as a hood ornament.

"You must have been up all night," I said, putting him into a headlock. I wanted to add, *I'm gonna miss you when I'm in Colorado*, but I didn't. Instead, I gave him a quick, hard noogie.

"Oh, you know us Dupres," Rémi said, "any excuse to work on a big project." He broke free of my grip, and we both cracked up. "Actually, the hardest part was keeping the noise down. We were sure you'd hear the music, come down to the barn, and want to join the party."

"Yeah?" I thought back to the previous night. "Where was I?"

"Probably trying to decide if you'll need a medium or large size U.S. team jersey."

I grabbed Rémi from behind, lifted him up off the ground, and spun him around in circles—like we used to do to each other as little kids. "I'm a Dupre," I said and stopped twirling before we both got too dizzy. "I'll definitely need a large."

Mémère wrapped her arms around our waists to help steady us. "Good things come in big, strong packages," she said and rested her head on my shoulder. "Not everyone is blessed with these genes."

I leaned into Mémère. "I'll make you proud."

She tightened her grip around my waist. "I already am."

Coach Roy tossed my bag into the back of his pickup, climbed behind the wheel, and fired up the engine. I opened the passenger side door, raised myself up on the running board, and looked out at everyone who had gathered for my good-bye. I wondered if the other girls traveling to ID Camp were getting this kind of send-off.

Pa stood on the edge of the crowd. I waved to him. He lifted his chin. I ran and threw my arms around him. "I love you, Pa. *Merci*."

He gently patted my back. "Be a good girl, Flora."

I lifted my necklace out from under my shirt, so only he could see the soccer ball. "I'm gonna make you and Ma proud," I said into his chest, and this time he hugged me. Hard.

On the short walk back to Coach's truck, I looked out at the brown fields, full of potatoes. I should have felt bad about leaving during Harvest Break, but I didn't. I felt like my family wanted this for me as much as I did. They finally seemed to understand my dream of playing soccer for the U.S.A.

Suddenly, a trumpet pierced the morning air. It was Rémi, first trumpet in the Acadia Central School band, standing atop the cab of the old red pickup.

Coach Roy looked at me. "Flora Dupre, are you ready to make a U.S. national soccer team?"

"YES!" everyone, including me, screamed.

I climbed into the truck. Pa slammed the door shut, gave

me a goofy smile, and then tapped me on the arm like he was playing a game of tag. He quickly stepped beyond my reach and said, "Last touch." When he said it, my mind flashed back to Ma, and how she used to do that when someone was going on a trip. She said it was for good luck. It scared me that I'd forgotten that. I didn't want to forget anything about Ma.

And then Uncle Henri's booming voice brought me back to the present. "U-S-A, U-S-A," he started, and pretty soon everyone was chanting those three beautiful letters at the top of their lungs.

The cold dirt crunched under Coach Roy's tires, and we were off. I hung out the passenger side window waving at my family and friends, straining to hear Rémi's trumpet blasts and the U-S-As.

I didn't pull myself into the cab until we'd bounced off the dirt road and onto the paved county road at the edge of the farm.

Here I come, U.S. Soccer, ready or not.

Chapter 10
BYOB

A tall boy with a Red Sox T-shirt stretched over his broad shoulders stood in front of me. "Excuse me," he said. "Do you know where the International Sports Academy bus stop is?" We were at baggage claim waiting for our bags. He was so cute all I could do was stare at him. His lips moved, but all I heard was blah, blah, blah. He pointed to the soccer ball in my hands. "I just figured you're going to the Academy."

"Good-looking and smart, too." *Did I just say that out loud?* From the look on his face, I had. I tried again. "Sorry," I said, "First time on a plane." *Flora!* I took a deep breath. "Yes, I'm going to the Academy, and no, I don't know where the bus is."

"That's cool," he said, flicking his head to get his bangs out of his eyes. "We'll figure it out together." When he looked at me with his blue eyes I felt a swarm of butterflies whip through my belly.

While we waited for our bags we sat on the floor near the rental car counters and got to know each other. Which, because I was still cringing from the "good-looking" comment, meant I basically kept my mouth shut and listened. His name was Logan Livingston; he was in the ninth grade and a nationally ranked pole-vaulter from Boston. This was his first trip to the ISA. We talked about the Red Sox and his parents' vacation house in Southern Maine, in Kennebunkport.

"Do you know the Bushes?" I asked, knowing darn well he wouldn't know the ex–Presidents of the United States, but they had a house in Kennebunkport, and I didn't know what else to say.

"Kinda," Logan said and shrugged his shoulders. "My dad does mostly. Golf, ya know." I smiled and nodded, like, *Oh sure, us Dupres, we're always hanging out with former world leaders and their families.* He slid his hand up under his shirt and revealed Abercrombie & Fitch–worthy abs. "I don't go up to Maine very much anymore because of training," he said.

Logan was the cutest boy I'd ever met. Ever. He was tall, he was athletic. I slapped myself out of it. "Ayuh," I said. "We don't get to Kennebunkport very often." Like, never.

The buzzer on the luggage belt sounded, and we jumped up and squeezed forward with everyone else. Once we'd gathered our bags and Logan's poles, we headed outside. When we saw the red, white, and blue International Sports Academy bus parked at the curb, I said, "That's wicked," and Logan burst out laughing. "What?" I said.

"It's just . . . It sounds so cute the way you say 'wicked'. . . . Say it again."

"Wicked," I said a little too loud.

Logan laughed. "We say wicked all the time in Boston, but it just sounds better with your accent." I made a funny face and he said, "No, I like it. It's wicked good. You're wicked cool. Look, the bus—wicked awesome." I didn't know if the cutest boy in the world was making fun of me, and I didn't care. "Trust me," he said. "It's cute."

You're cute, I thought. Logan stepped aside and made a grand sweeping motion with his arm. "Your chariot awaits." I boarded the bus with his hand squarely on my back and my heart racing.

The bus was packed with teenagers shouting back and forth at each other. I threw my backpack on the first open seat, right behind the driver, the only adult on the bus, and dragged my duffel to the back, where the seats had been replaced with luggage racks. It was clear that in addition to soccer players and pole-vaulters, there were figure skaters, tennis players, and archers on the bus. Just as I managed to wedge my duffel between two massive bags of tennis rackets, the bus lurched forward and I toppled into the back of another pole-vaulter. "Hey, watch it." He pointed at my feet. "Don't step on my poles."

That's when I looked down and realized the floor of the back of the bus was covered with hard, plastic tubes, many wrapped in colorful, padded bags. I felt like I was in a box of giant pick-up sticks, only they were vaulters' poles and, based on Angry Boy's reaction, very expensive. I tried to get a laugh out of him by exaggerating the movement of my feet as I moved among the tubes.

He gave me a look like, *You are the biggest dork*. I felt about an inch tall. *Thanks for the warm welcome.* I eased my way back up the aisle, but stopped when I felt Logan grab my arm. I felt my heart race again. Was he flirting with me? Would I even know what flirting looked like? "Hey, Flora." He was sitting with some boys he seemed to know from track meets. "What's the soccer thing you're here for?"

"National Development Identification Camp."

"Cool," he said, and I smiled as I continued toward my seat. I'd only been in Colorado a half hour and I'd already made a friend, a guy friend, who was cuter than all the boys at Acadia Central. Oh yeah, and he was taller than me, too.

The Rocky Mountains zipped by as we barreled down the highway. I'd only ever seen pictures of the Rockies. I pulled out my phone and started to type an e-mail to Mémère. I was telling her about the flight—the view, the turbulence, and of course, the food—when I heard something from a few rows back that made my stomach collapse.

"Who invited frizz head?"

I knew the girl wasn't talking about me, but instinctively I reached up and smoothed down my hair anyway. Then I went back to typing on my phone.

"Like someone that fat is going to make the team." It was a different girl's voice.

Fat? Okay, I wasn't fat. They were talking about someone—

"Yeah, what's up with bringing a soccer ball to camp?" said another girl.

I stopped rolling the ball around in my lap. There were three of them, but I didn't dare turn around. The last thing I wanted was for them to know I'd heard them.

"I guess I missed the part on the invitation that said BYOB—".

"Yeah, Bring Your Own Ball."

"That's hilarious, Tatiana."

"Yeah, hilarious."

The three girls dissolved into laughter. The boys sitting across from me looked around to see who they were talking about. I slid down in my seat ever so slightly, and rolled the ball off my lap and out of view of everyone else. I hugged my backpack to my chest and stared straight ahead.

For the remainder of the short bus ride to the Academy, I scrolled through my old e-mails—*why hadn't anyone from home sent me an e-mail yet?*—and tried not to hear the girls' ugly comments. But, me being a professional eavesdropper, I couldn't completely tune them out. As Mémère always said, know your enemies. The best I could piece together was that these girls were a) from different cities in California, b) teammates on the same Olympic Development Program team, c) shoo-ins to make the Under-15 U.S. Girls' National Team, and d) royal bitches. They went on and on about how they were going to be the forward line for the U-15s—Tatiana at center forward—*I don't think so, that's my position!*—and Kaylee and Zoe as her support strikers.

We'll see about that. In the meantime, I made a mental note to steer clear of Tatiana, Kaylee, and Zoe—who, from that moment on, were known to me as the Queens Bs.

When the bus came to a stop at the Academy, I stayed in my seat and pretended to search for something in the bottom of my backpack. I wanted to get a good look at these girls. When their three blonde ponytails swished past me, I fought the urge to stick out my foot and trip them.

Chapter 11
Wackadoodle

The other kids grabbed their bags and rushed in through the massive glass front doors, but I hung back. I'd been dreaming about the International Sports Academy for years, ever since I'd first read about it in *Sports Illustrated for Kids*. It was like the U.S. Olympic Training Center, but for kids. And not just any kids—you had to be one of the best athletes under the age of eighteen, in your sport, in your country, to get invited to the ISA. This wasn't some rich kids' sports academy where your parents could buy your way in—no, this was the real deal. You were invited to the ISA by national team coaches because they believed you had the potential to one day compete for your country in the World Championships and the Olympic Games.

I tilted my head back, closed my eyes, and did a little dance. I couldn't believe it, I was at the freakin' International Sports Academy. Me and a thousand other kids—pursuing our dreams of representing our countries on the world stage. I'd done my research. I knew that kids here specialized in twenty-six different summer Olympic sports, like soccer and gymnastics, and seven winter Olympic sports, like skiing and skating. This wasn't Soccerland. This was the ISA, and I was really here.

Standing outside the main entrance, the Academy looked like a university campus. Low-slung, red-brick dormitories spread out to my right. A series of gymnasiums with floor-to-ceiling windows hugged a hill to my left. Small wooden signs pointed toward an auditorium, dining hall, research laboratories, and offices. A group of modern, brown-shingled buildings, many linked together by glass walkways, lay nestled in huge tracts of freshly mown lawns. Snowcapped mountains lay off in the distance to the West.

I wanted to spin around like Julie Andrews in *The Sound of Music* and sing "The hills are alive . . ." with sports.

"What do you think?"

I jumped at the sound of the man's voice. I wanted to walk away, but I didn't know where to go, so I turned and answered him. "I think I'm dreaming," I said, "and nobody better wake me up."

I thought he'd laugh, but he didn't. He just scrunched up his face, took a step closer, and said, "So you're a dreamer?"

"I—I guess so," I said. "Well, I'm not a space shot, head-in-the-clouds dreamer, if that's what you mean." I shifted my eyes away from him and back to the two-story, A-frame main building with its massive glass doors. I was so happy to be at the ISA, I wasn't going to let this weirdo spoil it for me.

"What do you dream about?" he asked.

I figured I'd never see this man again, so I told the truth. "To play soccer for the U.S. Women's National Team in the World Cup and the Olympics." I took a breath. "To win gold medals."

He turned and stared at me. "Are you willing to do *any-thing* to make the U.S. team?"

"Ayuh, definitely. Anything," I said, before reconsidering my words. "Well, I'm not going to rob a bank, but yes, as long as it's legal, I'll do it."

He turned and walked toward the gymnasiums. Without looking at me, he called over his shoulder, "It's good to dream big, but remember this: you're not in Maine anymore, Flora Dupre. This is Oz, and I'm the almighty wizard."

I watched him walk away. *What a wackadoodle! Thanks for ruining my ooooh-aaaah-I'm-at-the-International-Sports-Academy moment.*

I reached down to pick up my bags, and then it hit me. He knew my name, that I was from Maine. But who was *he*?

Chapter 12

Hand Scans and a Woman Named Sally

By the time I reached the check-in desk, the other kids had been given their room assignments and had gone off to unpack. A tiny woman with a blonde mushroom cap hairdo sat behind the enormous half-moon desk. "And you must be Flora," she said and stood up, which made her seem shorter than when she was sitting down. "I'm Sally. Welcome to the International Sports Academy."

I shook her outstretched hand. *Finally someone nice*, I thought as I dropped my backpack onto the polished floor.

"Pull up a stool," she said and slid a small gray box toward me. It had a bunch of buttons on top and a cutaway on the bottom, where I could see the drawing of a hand. "Do me a favor," Sally said, "and put your hand on top of that outline." I slipped my right hand into the opening. "Use those little plastic pegs to keep your fingers apart." Sally pressed a couple of buttons, then asked me to enter a six digit secret code. I went for the obvious: August 1, 1996—Rémi's birthday and the day the U.S. women defeated China for the first Olympic gold medal in soccer. I typed in 811996, hit enter, and Sally said, "That's it."

I didn't know what "it" was, but I nodded politely, removed my hand, and continued to listen to Sally chatter away. In a matter of minutes, I'd heard her life story. She lived on the outskirts of town with her husband and two dogs, and worked most afternoons at the front desk. It didn't take a genius to figure out that Sally really loved to talk, almost as much as she loved her unofficial role as Academy mom.

Motormouth aside, there was something familiar and comforting about Sally. I'd only been at the Academy for fifteen minutes, and yet sitting with Sally, I felt as comfortable as I did back home at the kitchen table with Mémère.

Sally laid a map of the Academy—it looked like a small city—on the desktop and circled the Beijing wing, where I would live. "All the dorms are named after Olympic host cities," she said, "like Berlin, Montréal, Sydney, and Atlanta." I loved the idea of living in Beijing—it reminded me of Carli Lloyd's left-footed, overtime shot from twenty yards out that gave the U.S. women the gold medal over Brazil at the 2008 Beijing Olympics. I was still daydreaming about gold medals when I heard Sally say my roommate was Samantha Rhodes, an elite gymnast, who arrived yesterday for a one-month U.S. Gymnastics Junior National Team training camp.

"I think you two are going to hit it off. Samantha's a special one, and I can tell you are, too." Sally rolled her chair to the left so she could file my paperwork in a cabinet. When she was done she spun back toward me, rocketed the chair forward, and slapped her palms on the desk. "All righty then, off you go," she said. "And don't go too crazy at the ice-cream bar."

"There's an ice-cream bar?" I threw my hands in the air. "Okay, it's official. I'm never leaving this place."

Sally laughed and sent me on my way. I got halfway to Beijing before I realized she hadn't given me a room key. As Mémère would say, "If she'd spent a little less time jaw-wagging and a little more time doing her job . . ." I laughed at the thought of Mémère reprimanding Sally.

I dropped my bags in the glass passageway between the main building and Beijing. "I'll just be a minute," I said. "Don't go off exploring this place without me." I took a quick look around to make sure no one had heard me talking to my luggage and headed back to Sally's desk. I pulled out my phone and typed a quick e-mail to Mémère as I jogged through the hallways.

Arrived safely. Love it here! Have already met a wacka-doodle and a lady who talks more than you. ☺ xoxo

When I reached Sally, she said, "Sorry kiddo. With all my blabbing I forgot to tell you we don't use room keys here. Remember when I had you place your hand on that box and punch in a secret code? That was so we could get your hand-geometry into our security system—"

"Hand-geometry?" I felt my phone vibrate in my pocket. Mémère! I couldn't wait to read her response, but Sally was still jabbering away.

"The size and shape of your hand. The fancy name is biometric hand-geometry recognition." She rolled her eyes. "Anywho, around here we use handprints instead of photos to identify people. Keeps the place safer, especially with so many kids. So, to open your dorm room, or get into the dining hall, or whatever, just place your hand on the little gray box next to the door, punch in your secret code, and open sesame."

"Pretty fancy," I said.

"Only the best for you kids," Sally said and playfully shooed me away from the desk.

I yanked my phone out my pocket.

MA CHERIE! WE MISS YOU. TOO QUIET AROUND HERE. NIGHT NIGHT.

I laughed out loud. The caps lock key must have gotten stuck again. I didn't have the heart to tell Mémère she was screaming at me. I smiled thinking of everyone back home. I picked up my bags and headed toward the Beijing wing. Along the way I passed a couple of short, squat guys. Their jackets read Canada Junior Weightlifting Team. From a distance they looked like really muscular midgets. But when they got up close I realized they were about my age. I moved up against the wall to let them pass. I wanted to call out after them, *Oh boys, if that weightlifting thing doesn't work out, I know a potato farm in Maine that could use you.*

When I got to my room I did as Sally instructed, placed my hand on the gray box, punched in my secret code—which reminded me, I needed to e-mail Rémi—and the door popped open. "Wicked cool," I said and then stopped dead in my tracks. U.S.A. Gymnastics leotards and team sweats were draped over every surface of the right-hand side of the room. The left-hand side—clearly mine—was spotless. The sight of Samantha's U.S.A. gear made my belly fill with butterflies. I couldn't believe my roommate was on a *national* team.

I dragged my suitcase into the room and dropped my

backpack on the neatly made bed to my left. I felt something under my foot, looked down, realized I was standing on a U.S.A. Gymnastics T-shirt, and jumped backward. I felt like I'd just stepped on the American flag with muddy boots. I picked up the shirt, folded it, and laid it on Samantha's bed, but not before running my fingers over the raised U.S.A. letters. Goose bumps covered my arms.

ID Camp didn't start until the next morning, so I wasn't sure what to do with myself. I checked my phone, no messages, so I sent off quick e-mails to Rémi and Pa. Part of me wanted to find a net and kick my soccer ball around, but it was getting dark and I didn't know where the field was. I decided to spend some time exploring the Academy. In my wanderings I discovered weight lifting rooms, a rehab center, several gymnasiums, an indoor soccer field, ice rinks, an archery range, squash courts, a dining hall, and a movie theater. By the end of my tour, I felt like I'd walked for miles. And just when I thought I'd never find my way back to Beijing, I came around a corner and found myself in the main entryway where I'd checked in with Sally.

I reached up and touched Ma's soccer ball charm. "Ma," I said in my head. "I'm here. I'm really here at the ISA." I leaned against a wall and tried to take it all in. Dozens of kids in national team warm-ups speaking a gazillion different languages wandered through the main foyer toward the dining hall. I couldn't believe some kids actually got to live and train full-time at the Academy. This place made Acadia look like a cowpoke town. And then I realized, Acadia *was* a cowpoke town. But it was my cowpoke town.

I glanced at my phone. No messages. Why hadn't anyone

written back? I shoved the phone in my pocket. I was lonely and a little bit homesick, but mostly I was nervous. I touched the soccer ball charm again. I could live with being nervous, especially with an ice-cream bar.

Chapter 13
Punch Fronts and Stinky Clothes

When I returned to my room and popped open the door, a pipsqueak of a girl, all brown eyes, ponytail, and bright white teeth, bounced forward. "No keys," she said. "How cool is this place?"

So *this* was Samantha. I looked toward the heavens and thanked the roommate gods.

While I unpacked, Samantha talked . . . and talked. I tried to remember everything, but—good gravy—she was a fast talker. She'd just turned thirteen and was an elite—the highest level—gymnast. There were only about one hundred elite gymnasts in the United States. She'd just become a Junior International Elite and was at the ISA trying to make the U.S. team for the upcoming Pacific Rim Championships, which, she said, would put her in a good position to make the Youth Olympic Games team. Samantha's dad was some big-shot general in the air force; his career took Samantha's family all over the world. She'd lived in Japan, Germany, Turkey, Korea, and Australia. A few months ago, her father was transferred to an air force base in Oklahoma, which worked well for Samantha because she was able to train in Norman at the gym of Olympic gold medalists Bart Conner and Nadia Comaneci.

When there was a slight break in the conversation, I said, "Boys-oh-boys. It's hard to get a word in edgewise with you." I had to wonder, were all gymnasts this hyper?

"Sorry," Samantha said. "I'm just wired from training today. I really, really, really needed to hit my punch front out of my final tumbling pass. And I did."

"Punch front?"

"What'd you say—boys-oh-boys—I like that. Hey we've got a lot to learn about each other's sports, don't we? Come by the gym some time, and I'll show you a punch front."

Our room was smaller than my room back in Acadia, but it didn't feel small, even with Samantha bouncing all over the place. When I pulled out the drawers beneath my bed, Samantha jumped to her feet. "Okay, whatever you do, don't store stinky workout clothes in the drawer under your head." She held her nose, pretended to be woozy, and flopped onto her bed. "Been there, done that. Not pretty."

"Got it," I said. "Stinky clothes go in the drawer to the right of my feet." And we both laughed.

Samantha pointed toward the large bureau to the right of the window. "I figured I'd be the short roommate, so I filled the bottom two drawers and left the top two for you." We arranged our toothbrushes, sunscreen (me), and glitter eyeshadow (Samantha) on the shelf over the small sink in the corner.

"Ah, finally," I said when the last bits were unpacked and the empty bags shoved into the back of the closet. We both collapsed on our beds.

"We're gonna be super-best roommates," Samantha said.

"Ayuh." I had a gut feeling about Samantha. Sure, she was a talker, and I wondered if she ever chilled out, but bottom line, I trusted her. And that was a relief, especially after my awful bus ride and running into that weird guy. I lay back on my pillow and stared at the ceiling. "So I met these horrible girls on the bus from the airport."

"Oooooh do tell," Samantha said as she stretched her left leg toward the ceiling.

I told her all about the Queen Bs. Didn't leave anything out. Except the part about making fun of me for bringing a soccer ball to camp.

"There are always kids like that at the Academy." Samantha picked at a callous on her left hand. "I've been coming here since I was nine. Trust me, *everyone* thinks they're national team material." She raised her right leg toward the ceiling. "Little secret, the ones who brag the most never make the team."

"Really?"

"Definitely."

"That's good to hear," I said and tried to extend my leg like Samantha's. "Ow. How do you do that?"

"Freak of nature," she said, and we both giggled.

I gave up on the gymnastics stretches and said, "I guess I'm just not used to kids like that. I come from a really small school. Don't get me wrong, it's not like everyone's perfect in Acadia, it's just, when you grow up with the same ten kids in your grade, you learn to get along."

"Wait. Ten kids? You mean in your class, right?"

"Class, grade, same thing. There's only one class per grade. Ten's huge." I yawned and rolled over on my stomach. "Last year's seniors only had six kids."

"That sounds kind of cool."

"Actually, it is." I sat up and leaned my back against the wall. "We're more like brothers and sisters than classmates."

Samantha returned to stretching her left leg. "You're lucky," she said. "We've moved around so much because of the military that I don't feel like anywhere is home. Well, except for the gym. Gyms are gyms, you know. As long as they have all four apparatus I'm good."

"That's how I feel about soccer fields. Green, brown, I don't care as long as there's a ball and a goal. Oh, and speaking of soccer, I met the weirdest man today."

"Oooooh another story."

After I told Samantha my mystery man story, she swung her legs off the bed and onto the floor. "Creepy. He knew your name? And that you're from Maine?"

"I hope I never see him again. He was just so . . . intense."

Samantha pulled a pillow over her head and peeked out at me. "That's kind of spooky, don't you think?"

"I know what my grandmother would say, 'There goes another wackadoodle. Just hope he doesn't cross your path again.'" We laughed. "Of course, when it comes to wacka-doodles, Mémère's usually talking about crazy chipmunks or rabid skunks."

Samantha held up three fingers on each hand. "Wacka-doodle be gone."

"What's that? Some Girl Scout thing?"

"Nah, I just made it up. But it's gonna work, trust me."

That night, while Samantha slept, I slipped out of bed and walked to the window. Most kids at the Academy preferred rooms on the west side of the dorms because you could see the Rocky Mountains from there, but I liked the eastern view. Technically we looked out onto a parking lot, but we also looked toward Maine.

I leaned close to the window, so close my breath left a foggy patch. I traced a heart in it with my finger. "Pa?" I whispered. *"Merci."*

Chapter 14
One Hundred Girls

The next morning, I climbed to the top of the hill behind the gymnasiums and discovered the most wonderful sight: six perfectly manicured soccer fields. Laid side by side and end to end, they formed a magnificent green quilt, complete with benches that, if you squinted, looked like the big white hand-stitches on Mémère's quilts.

A huge group of girls had gathered at the base of the hill, while a dozen or so adults, decked out in red, white, and blue U.S. Soccer gear, mingled near the benches. "Holey moley," I said and swallowed hard. My bacon and eggs were trying their best to come back up. I should have followed Samantha's lead and had oatmeal with bananas, but it was too late now.

A short, muscular African American girl stopped next to me and said, "Pretty cool, right?"

I turned and said, "I think I'm gonna barf."

The girl laughed as she struggled in the wind to gather what seemed like hundreds of long, skinny braids into one massively poofy ponytail.

"No, I'm serious," I said.

"You'll be fine," she replied. "I'm Nikesha."

"Sorry," I said, "I'm Flora. It's nice to meet you." We stared at the scene below us.

"I heard they invited one hundred girls, but from up here it looks like more, doesn't it?"

"Ayuh." *A hundred girls*, I thought, *and three Queen Bs.* Thinking of them, and seeing the totally professional training setup, I was glad I'd gone with my gut and left my Acadia soccer ball back in the room. No way did I want to be made fun of again by the Queen Bs.

Nikesha smacked me on the back and out of my pity party. "Come on, let's go show these wimpy little twerps what we've got." She took off running down the hill, her ponytail flying and her shoes kicking up freshly cut grass. I admired Nikesha's spirit, but I was still dealing with the bacon and eggs situation in my belly, so I walked down the hill.

At field level, I stuck to the edges of the group. There was lots of screaming and hugging going on. Loads of girls seemed to know each other from regional camps and tournaments. The Queen Bs had stationed themselves at the midfield line, like dogs marking their territory. *Squirt. Mine! Squirt, squirt. Mine!* They were making a big show of juggling balls off their thighs, feet, and heads—like we couldn't *all* do that stuff. I didn't give them the satisfaction of watching. I plopped myself down as far away from them as possible on a patch of grass near the touchline.

I loosened up my muscles with gentle stretches and listened to the conversations going on around me. No one talked about high school teams; it was all club this, club that. And it seemed like everyone played in the Olympic Development

Program. *Please don't anyone ask me what ODP team I play for.* I tried to make myself invisible. And then I stopped myself. I belonged at ID Camp. Well, I thought I did. The coaches wouldn't have invited me if I didn't. Would they? I didn't know what to believe. I hoped it was simply first-day jitters. I decided the safest thing to do was keep my mouth shut and fly under the radar.

With everyone mingling around it was impossible to figure out who was in charge. All the coaches had clipboards and whistles, but nobody looked like the big cheese. I was coaxing my right quadriceps into a hurdler's stretch when a slender girl stopped next to me. She had the most perfect posture I'd ever seen. She stood about five feet but seemed much taller. Her straight, light brown hair was swept back into a sleek ponytail, and everything she wore was color-coordinated—from her headband (lavender), to her shorts and tank top (purple, lavender, and white), to her socks. She even had lavender laces in her soccer shoes and a purple backpack. She looked like something right out of the L.L.Bean catalog. Girls' Athletic Gear, page 46.

I, on the other hand, had on a faded pair of blue Umbro shorts and an extra-large Acadia cotton T-shirt. Next to Her Perfectness, I felt about as attractive as a fly on a horse's butt. She stretched and every so often flipped her ponytail, like, hey, annoying fly, go away. I couldn't stop watching her. Sure, it was rude, but she was like *Seventeen* magazine's idea of a soccer player. Perfect skin, perfect clothes, perfect everything.

After about five minutes of silently stretching side by side, I got up the nerve to speak to Matchy-Matchy-Perfect-Girl. "Hi. I'm—I'm Flora."

She stood up, turned her head two degrees toward me and said, "Sperry."

Sp—what?

She stared straight ahead, pulled her right heel toward her butt. Her balance didn't waver. I would've said, *Nice to meet you*, but Sperry clearly wasn't looking for friends, so I just kept sneaking glances at her out of the corner of my eye. She seemed so confident and comfortable keeping to herself. When I started getting intimidated by how she applied sunscreen, I told myself to get a grip. I heard a little voice in my head say, "Maybe Sperry's just as nervous as you, but she's hiding behind her perfect girl facade."

Yeah, right.

Perfect Girl turned her back to me, like she could hear my thoughts, and that's when I noticed she had moles. A lot of them. So many that I started to count the little brown raised spots on her arms and shoulders . . . 21, 22, 23—

A light tap on my foot snapped me out of my mole obsession. "Good morning, Dorothy. Enjoying Oz?" I looked up, and it was him. I heard Mémère whisper, "Oh, no. Wackadoodle alert."

I didn't say anything, just half-smiled at him, the way I would have smiled at a crazy person on the streets of New York City—if I'd ever been to New York City.

The only thought that ran through my head was, *Please tell me you're not part of this camp.*

But it was obvious he was.

Chapter 15
I'm the Boss

A coach's whistle blew. "All right, girls, gather 'round. We're going to get started."

I tried to hang on the edge, but Nikesha had other ideas. She grabbed my hand and dragged me to a spot in the middle of the group. Everyone sat in a semicircle on the grass around the cluster of coaches.

The wackadoodle climbed up on a bench and pulled out a clipboard. I turned to the girl on my left and asked, "Who's that?"

Before she could respond, Nikesha leaned over and said, "Girl, what rock have you been living under?" This Nikesha chick was a bit bossy for my taste. I felt like saying, "Did I ask you?"

But when Nikesha said, "That's Matt Keene. He's the U-15 Girls' National Team coach," I almost fainted.

The head coach? *Okay, calm down, maybe he's not as weird as he seems.*

"Welcome to ID Camp. I'm Matt Keene, and I'm the one

who will ultimately decide if you get to play for the U.S.A. any-time soon. You can call me Matt or Coach, but I want to make one thing clear, I'm not here to be your friend. You want hugs and warm fuzzies, don't come looking for them from me."

Off to my left, I saw Tatiana mouth "whatever" to Kaylee, who in turn flashed an L on her forehead.

I had a lot of trouble following Matt's voice. "Nikesha," I said. "What's his accent?"

"He's British. You've really got to listen, don't you?"

"Ayuh."

We turned our attention back to Matt. "Okay, just so we're all clear, I'm the boss and your future lies in my hands. Any questions?"

A couple of girls laughed, but I was pretty sure Matt wasn't joking. Or offering to do a question and answer session.

Matt stepped down from the bench and paced back and forth in front of us as he talked. "It's a given, you're all ex-cellent soccer players. That's why we invited you here." The Queen Bs nodded their heads in unison. "What we're looking for in the next two weeks is not so much how your bodies play, but how your *minds* play soccer."

Tatiana turned to Zoe. "Why doesn't he just shut up so we can play?"

Matt stopped in front of Tatiana. "Ms. Markova, it appears you have difficulty paying attention."

Tatiana opened her eyes wide, all fake innocent. "What?"

"Lass, how about you step to the side and do crunches until I'm done?" Tatiana took her time getting up. "Crack on," he said. Her cheeks turned bright red. I covered my mouth to hide my smile. "We're waiting."

Without removing her eyes from Matt, the girl next to me

said, "Score one for the boss man."

It hit me then. I was in the big time now. This wasn't Maine high school soccer. This was the first step to playing in the Olympics and the World Cup. This was what Ma and I had fantasized about. I was close enough to touch it. All I had to do was convince Matt Keene—*not* my friend—that I was national team material.

Chapter 16
Best Swag Ever

The coaches divided us into small groups, threw out some balls, and had us play a series of small sided games. It was a blast. They let us choose our positions, so of course, I sprinted to the midfield line and snagged my usual spot at center forward. It felt so good to play. I was comfortable up front. Looking around, I knew I wasn't the best forward at camp, but I held my own. The only thing I was nervous about was trying to remember the other girls' names. So many of them seemed to know each other. It was a change for me to be the outsider on a soccer field. In Maine, everybody knew who I was.

The coaches stood on the touchlines helping to make calls and retrieving balls when they went out of bounds, but mostly they kept quiet and watched. Coach Roy had told me they might do this. "The coaches will be watching you from the minute you arrive at the academy," he'd said. "There's nothing casual or random about choosing a national team." And Coach Roy was right. The coaches, especially Matt, seemed to see everything, especially the girls who fooled around or trash-talked. I wanted Matt to notice me for my work ethic, my attitude, and my skills, so I kept quiet and did what I knew best; I played soccer.

After a couple of hours of rotating us in and out of a series of 3 v. 3 (three girls per side) and 5 v. 5 (five girls per side) games, Matt called us together and announced, "Let's go get your gear."

It took a moment for me to register what he meant, but when I did, I realized those were the five most beautiful words I'd ever heard.

All one hundred of us hot and sweaty girls jammed into a training room to get our official Nike gear for camp. Long tables had been placed together to form a large L; staff members stood behind the tables, and in back of them were dozens of boxes of clothes and shoes.

This was the first time any of us had been issued official U.S.A. gear. Even the Queen Bs came down off their high horses to mingle with the peons.

Zoe turned to me—*me!*—and said, "This is the same exact gear the Women's National Team wears."

"I thought they were just gonna give us pinnies," I said, and we both laughed.

"Zoe," Tatiana said from across the room, in a tone that meant, *Come here!*

Zoe looked at me and rolled her eyes. "Sorry," she whispered and walked toward Tatiana and Kaylee.

I hadn't realized making new friends was going to be as hard as making the U-15s, but like Matt said, we weren't here for the warm fuzzies.

Each of us was assigned a jersey number from 1–100, which we'd wear for the duration of camp. Some of the girls

angled for the jersey numbers of current national team players, but I didn't care what number I got. The jersey itself was
the most important thing. As I looked around the room, I
couldn't help but think how much Ma would have loved this.

While we waited not-so-patiently in line, I watched Nikesha poke Sperry in the ribs. "Hey," she said, a little louder than
necessary, "I bet you've bought ten national team jerseys, and
they're all hanging in your closet back home."

For the first time all day Sperry smiled. "I only have Mia
Hamm's and Julie Foudy's."

"What? You only like *retired* players?"

"No," Sperry said and then ducked her head a little. "I just
think it would be weird to wear a jersey of someone I might
actually get to play side by side with one day."

Nikesha raised her hand, and Sperry jumped backward.
When she realized Nikesha wasn't going to smack her, Sperry
completed the high five. "I like the way you think, Sperry-
monster."

Sperry said, "Thanks?" even though she still looked a bit
terrified that Nikesha was going to haul off and clobber her.

"I want *you* to be on my team," Nikesha said and threw
her arm around Sperry, who flinched before relaxing into
Nikesha's embrace.

I looked away—embarrassed by my own jealousy—wish-
ing someone had asked me to be on their team.

When it was my turn to step up to the tables, I stopped
stressing about all the new friendships that were springing up
around me. All I could think was, *This is really happening.
I'm going to walk out of this room with the full U.S. Soccer
National Team training gear uniform.*

"Small, medium, large, or should I just pinch you?" It was

Rainey, one of the Region 1 coaches from the Boston Olympic Development Program team.

"Um . . ."

"Take a breath. We'll figure it out." Rainey handed me a jersey. "Here. Try this one."

I slipped the blue short-sleeved jersey over my head, but it wouldn't go over my shoulders. Rainey yanked it back and tossed me the next size. That one fit perfectly. "Good thing red, white, and blue are your colors," she said.

I ran my hands up and down the silky fabric. "You think?"

"I *know*," Rainey said. "Hey, Flora, I haven't had a chance to tell you, but I'm psyched you were able to make it to camp on such short notice. We were so bummed you couldn't play for our Boston ODP this fall, but everybody understood. You can't help that you live in the boonies."

"Maine isn't the boo . . . yeah, it is." I laughed as I pulled on a pair of blue shorts. "I wish I could have played in Boston." I traced the U.S. Soccer patch on the right pant leg with my fingers. "I just can't believe I'm here."

Rainey and I continued to talk as I tried on warm-ups and wet-weather gear. When she handed me new footwear I said, "Oh man, cleats, too?"

"You want to be a real soccer player, you call these babies *boots*, okay? Never cleats."

"Boots—good." I said dragging out the oo's. "Boots—wicked good."

When Rainey told me we had to wear this gear for the rest of camp, I put my hands on my hips and pretended to pout. "Man, you've got a lot of rules around this place." I held up one of the T-shirts. "Guess you're gonna make me use this for a nightgown."

"You wouldn't be the first," Rainey said and stuffed the last items into my bag. "You're all set."

"No, I'm not. You still haven't pinched me."

Rainey leaned over the table and gently pinched my right triceps. "For good luck," she said. "Off you go, muscle girl."

I walked past a group of girls, where Nikesha was holding court. "I knew my mom named me Nikesha for a reason. Look at me." I watched Nikesha dance in a circle. "All decked out in my own brand."

The other girls laughed, but all I could think was, her mother didn't name her after a pair of shoes. *Did she?*

I followed Nikesha and her group toward the exit, our team bags overflowing with the world's best soccer swag, when one of the assistant coaches called out. "Girls, did you get your casual gear?"

We looked at each other and screamed. Nikesha, pretending to sound very grown-up and serious, said, "Why, no, we didn't."

"Hop in that line, and we'll get you sorted."

Nikesha flipped through an imaginary appointment book, then turned to me. "I hadn't planned on being here so long."

I smiled, happy to be noticed by her again. "I know," I said pretending to commiserate, "but we might as well stay, you know, since we're already here."

Nikesha slapped me on the back, grabbed my arm, and pulled me over to join Sperry, who was already in the casual gear line. Was I part of the cool group? We dissolved into a screaming, dancing trio. I think I was.

On our way back to the dorms, I glanced at my phone. An e-mail! From Rémi. Finally.

So? Are you a medium or a large?

I laughed so hard, I snorted. Which, when I saw Sperry's expression, I instantly regretted. "What's so funny?" she asked.

"My cousin," I said. "I think he has mental telepathy." Sperry was tiny, skinny. How could I explain that needing a size large uniform was funny in my family? "It's like he knew we were getting our gear today."

"Weird," she said. "Even *we* didn't know we were getting gear." I nodded, hoping she didn't think *I* was weird. "So you guys are close?"

"Kind of—he's more like a brother than a cousin." *Even if I can't really talk to him about soccer*, I wanted to add. "Do you have a lot of cousins?"

"A couple," she said. "But I never see them. I don't really know them."

I had no idea what to say to that. My cousins were such a big part of my life. So I changed the subject to something we both felt comfortable talking about: Soccer.

Chapter 17
Pa? Can You Hear Me?

Once I'd dragged both large travel bags into my room, I laid everything out on the bed. The final tally included:

- 1 pair soccer boots
- 1 pair running shoes
- 4 team shorts
- 4 training jerseys
- 1 warm-up suit
- 1 rain suit
- 4 pairs socks
- 2 T-shirts
- 4 sports bras
- 1 pair flip-flops
- 1 sweatshirt
- 2 baseball caps
- 2 casual shorts
- 2 casual long pants
- 4 shirts
- 2 jackets
- 1 sports watch

When I looked at all those red, white, and blue clothes, I couldn't help but think of Acadia Central's green polyester uniforms. One pair of shorts and a jersey. Hand-me-downs from the boys' varsity.

I ran my fingers over my new boots. I'd only been at the Academy for one day, but I felt different. Grown-up. Independent. But I was also worried. Worried about messing up at ID Camp and never getting another chance to try out for a national team.

I sat in the desk chair, laid my head back, closed my eyes, and slowly spun 'round and 'round. The more I spun the more I thought about my future. About soccer. No one from Acadia had ever been a professional athlete or competed in the Olympics. But I'd known forever that that's what I wanted to do. Ma understood. *Follow your dream, no matter what.* That's what she'd said, but in Acadia, national-level soccer was just a dream, it wasn't really possible. At the ISA, everywhere I looked, kids were on national teams. This was *real*.

I stopped spinning. Grabbed my phone and called Pa. On the third ring he picked up, but all I could hear on the other end was the tractor.

"Allô? Allô?" I heard the tractor slowly shutting down. "Pa? You there?"

"Who's this?" The tractor made one last spluttery groan.

Seriously, who's this? Pa must have been the only person in the world who didn't check caller ID when his phone rang. "It's your *daughter*. Remember me?"

"Flora?" *Like you've got another daughter.* "How was the flight?"

"Fine," I said, but the flight felt like a million years ago. "Pa, the International Sports Academy, it's . . . incredible—"

"Gettin' cold here."

"Ayuh." I tried again. "Everyone is wicked nice. My room-mate's Samantha. She's one of the best gymnasts in the U.S. She's competed, like, everywhere. China. Australia. France. Even Argentina. I don't even know where Argentina is, except it's really far away."

"It's at the bottom of South America. Did you know they speak Spanish, English, German, and French there?" Clearly, Pa had been watching the National Geographic Channel too much.

"Ah, I do now."

"Pickin's going good. Rémi's working hard."

I tried again. "Pa, I can't believe some kids get to live here full-time—"

"Don't go getting any ideas—"

"No. Of course not," I said. "It's just, it's, well, it's like a dream being here. Oh! They gave us our uniforms today, and they're the same *exact* ones the U.S. Women's National Team wears for training. Can you believe it?" He didn't say anything. "Pa?" I looked at my phone. I'd heard some of the other kids talk about how crappy the cell reception was because of the mountains. "Pa, can you hear me?"

"Ayuh," he said.

"Okay, well, I just wanted to check in. It sounds like you're busy." There was so much more I wanted to tell him. Couldn't he *see* that?

"Well, be good, Flora."

"I miss you."

"Ayuh." The phone went dead.

"I love you, Flora," I said to myself. "I love you, too, Pa." I snapped the phone shut and flung it at my pillow.

I hopped off the chair and looked at the loot spread across my bed. I wasn't going to let Pa's moodiness ruin my day. I picked up an armful of clothes and inhaled their new clothes' scent. I strapped the heart rate monitor around my chest, just below the band of my sports bra, slipped the heart rate watch on my wrist, took a deep, relaxing breath, and pressed the start button. I looked at my heart rate:

70 beats per minute

I walked to the bed and lay down on top of my national team gear. I raised my wrist and looked at the readout on the watch:

85 beats per minute

Ayuh, it's the little things that make a girl's heart race.

Chapter 18
Football 101

That afternoon we gathered again at the soccer fields.

"Right, football 101," Matt said. "Football's all about making creative choices." He paused to look around. "Yeah, I'm gonna say football because that's what the sport's called where I come from. Get over it." A couple of the other coaches laughed. Clearly they'd heard Matt's rant on soccer versus football before. Matt glanced at them, and they wiped the smiles off their faces. "It's up to you girls as players to solve problems as they come up on the field," he said. "Coaches can scream and yell all we want, but we can't come out onto the pitch and make you do anything. It's not enough to have physical skills." He pointed to his head. "You need to use your brain and anticipate what could happen, over and over and over again."

Every eye on the field was focused on Matt.

"You're at a crossroads in your development as players. To step up from club teams to the U-15 Girls' National Team, you need to learn how to play creatively—how to make choices and take chances."

Nikesha, sitting in front of me with a couple of girls I hadn't met yet, turned around, caught my eye, and we smiled at each other. "Are you ready to step up?" she whispered. I nodded yes.

"Me, too," she said and low-fived me. "In my new official team gear." All the girls around us giggled.

Matt was still on his pulpit. "Let's take a survey," he said. "Now, be honest. How many of you are the best player on your team?"

One hundred hands shot up. Everyone, coaches and athletes, burst out laughing.

"It's nice to see modesty isn't a problem with this group," Rainey said.

Matt nodded. "Okay, how many of you feel it's up to you, and you alone, to solve problems as they come up during games?"

This time, pretty much everyone, except the goalies, raised their hands.

"Those days are over," Matt said. "Why? Because individuals don't win international level games, groups do. To make the U-15s you need to show us you can play as part of a group, that you can turn to your teammates and solve problems together."

Tatiana nodded at Kaylee and Zoe, convinced they had the group thing down. I wanted to slap the smug look off her face, but I was too captivated by what Matt was saying. "We've gathered you girls here to determine who has the ability to think like a national team player. Your assignment for the next two weeks is to play smart soccer. I could care less if you can bend it like Beckham—"

A girl to my left, I think her name was Hanna, whispered

into my ear. "Matt coached Beckham at Manchester United."

"*Beckham*, Beckham?"

"Yup."

Matt jumped down off the bench. "What I want to see from you girls is how clever you are." With that he let us loose again to play a series of 3 v. 3 and 5 v. 5 games for a couple of hours. Coach Roy told me to expect a lot of small sided games at ID Camp—he said 5 v. 5 was a good way for coaches to see how well players control the ball. I played on the front line again, mostly with Kaylee—*ugh*—and Tatiana—*double ugh*. Zoe, *lucky girl*, was assigned to another field. The Queen Bs didn't pass to me—big surprise—so I had to hustle and get the ball on my own. Not the ideal way to start camp, but whatever, I wasn't going to let their bitchiness stop me from showing the coaches how well I could play.

At one point I looked up and noticed Logan and some of his buddies watching from the sidelines. I hadn't spoken to Logan since the bus ride from the airport. What was it about that boy? He was probably on his way back to the dorms from the track, but I pretended he'd made a special detour to watch me. *Yeah, right.* But a few minutes later when I faked out Hanna with an awesome double scissors and then fired one into the goal, I heard him yell, "Good shot, Flora."

I gave him a wave, like, *I'm so freakin' cool I barely noticed you were watching.*

Once we'd all had a snack and something to drink, we were sent to one of the gymnasiums for physiological testing. Rainey said U.S. Soccer didn't usually do this kind of testing at U-14 Girls' National Team ID Camps, but the Academy's trainers needed to collect data for a study they were doing on young athletes; so for the rest of the afternoon, we were their guinea pigs.

Rainey assured us the tests had nothing to do with choosing the U-15 team, but no one believed her. We competed like it was the Olympics, to see how fast we could weave through a series of cones, run twenty-five and fifty meters, and how far we could jump vertically and horizontally. The trainers put us up on massage tables and measured our flexibility. I got all ticklish when Tony, the head trainer, pulled my leg around to measure the suppleness of my hip. "I feel like a giant pretzel," I said.

"That's good, it means you're limber," he said. "As you get older you're going to have to work hard to stay that way, otherwise you'll be more likely to get injured."

The final test of the day was done in a huge water tank. The trainers put each of us onto what looked like a giant vegetable scale and one at a time dunked us underwater to measure our body fat. "We usually use little metal pincers, called calipers, to measure body fat," Tony said. "But today we're doing a special study of body composition underwater. It's called hydrostatic weighing." He waved as he lowered me into the water. Just before my head dipped underwater he said, "Thanks for getting wet in the name of science."

You're welcome, I thought as my ears filled with water, and I forced as much air as possible from my lungs.

In Acadia, I was by far the best athlete, boy or girl. At ID Camp, I was definitely one of the top athletes, but for the first time in my life I was becoming known more for my size than anything else. And that bugged me. My whole life I'd been told, "You're a big, strong Dupre girl," like it was a good thing, but after an afternoon of testing I wasn't particularly proud of my bigness. After my underwater test, I dried myself off and grabbed my bag, but Rainey stopped me before I could slip out the door. "Hey, kiddo," she said. "Got a sec?"

"Sure." Unlike ole wackadoodle, Rainey was warm. And fuzzy. Like a cool older sister.

She put her hand on my elbow, steered me into a private office, and closed the door. "Why the long face?" she said.

"It's kind of embarrassing." Rainey didn't say anything, just looked at me. "It's . . . I'm feeling kind of *huge* next to the other girls."

Rainey laughed. "Well, next to them, you *are* huge." I opened my eyes wide. "Flora, that's a good thing."

"It is?" I said.

"Your size is part of the reason we invited you to camp. We can't win World Cups and Olympics without big, powerful girls like you." Rainey lifted my bag off my shoulder and set it on the ground, then she cupped my face in her hands. "Flora, you are what you are. You're tall. You're strong. And you're aggressive. The sooner you embrace it, the faster you'll move up in the system."

"But I'm fat." I thought back to Tatiana's words on the bus.

"Fat?" Rainey wrapped her arms around me, and I buried my cheek in her fleece vest. "Trust me, you're not fat. U.S. Soccer doesn't need fat players; we need strong, muscular players."

But I'm fat.

Rainey held me just far enough away from her so she could see my face. "Flora, don't give me one of those I-hear-you-but-I-don't-believe-you smiles." I re-jiggered my smile ever so slightly. She seemed pleased. "You know that body fat test we did?" she asked.

"Ayuh." *Don't remind me.*

"Only five girls have less body fat than you." Rainey realized I didn't follow what she was saying. "Let's try this another way. Have you ever heard the expression muscle weighs more than fat?"

"Of course."

"Well, you, Flora Dupre are living, breathing, soccer-playing proof of it. You're chock-full of muscle." She grabbed hold of my arms. "The next time you feel fat, just remember, ninety-four of those girls out there are fatter than you."

"Oh—"

"That's right. Now go get something to eat."

Chapter 19
Butterflies

On my way to the dining hall for dinner I called home. While I waited for someone to answer, I tried to imagine what was going on at that precise moment back on the farm. Pépère and Pa were probably watching TV in the living room while Mémère cleaned up the dinner dishes. I could almost smell one of her pies. Probably apple.

"Allô?" I heard dishes clinking in the background and laughed.

"Bonsoir Mémère. C'est Flora. Ça va?"

"Alors! Ma petite fleur," she said. "Your Pa told me you called him this afternoon."

"Ayuh," I said. I wanted to add: *Did he tell you what a bad mood he was in?*

"Flora," Mémère said. "I want to hear about everything. Every single thing. Let me turn the water off and sit down."

Mémère and I talked for nearly an hour. I told her everything. Everything I wanted to tell Pa. I knew she'd tell him, but still, it wasn't the same. It didn't make it okay. But, I had to admit it was comforting to hear Mémère's voice. "I didn't expect it to be so hard," I told her, "to make friends."

"Here's a little trick," Mémère said. "When you meet someone, make a point to remember her name. Then when you see her be sure to call her by name. Even if you've never been introduced to a girl, but you know her name, just act like you've already met."

"Really?"

"Ayuh, you'll be the most popular girl at the International Sports Academy before you know it."

"I don't need to be the most popular, I just want to fit in—"

"Oh, sweetheart, do you know how proud we are of you?" *Pa, too?* I wondered. "Pépère's been bragging to everyone in town. He's down at the barn right now. He sure is gonna be sorry he missed your call."

"Give him my love. I miss you, Mémère." Suddenly I was homesick. Really homesick. "I miss your pie."

She laughed. "Got an apple one sitting right here on the counter."

I held back the tears. "Save me a piece," I said.

"Hogwash. I'll bake you a fresh one the day you get home," she said. "This is probably costing a fortune, so I'll say good—"

Mémère was still living in the Dark Ages. No matter how many times we tried to explain unlimited calling plans she still thought you paid for phone calls by the minute. "—Mémère. Wait." I hesitated. "How's Pa?"

"He's fine, dear."

"This afternoon . . . he sounded sad. Again."

I heard her suck in her breath. "Don't you worry about that."

But I did. "Mémère, it's like he didn't even want to talk to me. Didn't want to hear all about camp and the academy."

"Oh, sweetheart. He just misses you. We all do. You know we love you. And we're proud of you."

I sighed. "I miss you, too. Give Pa and Pépère a big hug for me."

"Will do. And keep those e-mails coming. *À plus tard!*"

I shut my phone. Stared at it. Why couldn't *Pa* have told me he was proud of me?

I decided to e-mail Rémi. He was good at pulling me out of a bad mood. I opened my phone back up and started to type.

Out of nowhere I heard a boy's voice singing my name. "Flora-Flora-Flora-Flora!" And then I felt Logan grab me around the neck and wrestle me to the ground. "What's sha-kin' my Maine blueberry?" He held me in a playful headlock.

"Just calling home," I said, a little out of breath. He smelled *so* good. "Checkin' in."

"Ugh," he said as he released his grip from around my neck and flopped on his back next to me on the carpet. "I feel your pain." Our fingers, well, my pinkie and his thumb, touched briefly.

You do? "It's hard, right?" I said.

"You have to call home and say, 'Yes, Mom, I got here fine. They're feeding me, I'm getting lots of sleep and, yes, I'm washing behind my ears.'"

"And, 'I'm not wearing hole-y underwear.'" I felt my cheeks flush. *Flora!*

We both laughed. "Right?" Logan brushed his thumb against my pinkie, ever so gently. Twice. "I mean, I love my mom, but she drives me crazy on the phone. She asks a million questions. She wants to know how I spend every single minute of my day when I'm away from home. I try to get away with e-mails, but she wants to hear my voice. What am I— eight?"

I laughed. "Ayuh, my dad's the same way. It's so annoying." *Liar.*

A tall, blond surfer-type guy suddenly appeared above us. "Logan!" He nudged Logan's foot with his own. "Rockin' the ladies! What's up, my brother?"

Logan stood up. "Flora, Jason. Jason, Flora."

Jason offered his hand and pulled me up. When we were standing side by side, he said, "Tall, much?"

Great. Thanks for pointing out my freakish height.

Logan uttered, "Not cool," under his breath at Jason. Then he turned to me and said, "So, I'll see ya later?"

I smiled, like what Jason said hadn't bothered me.

When they'd gotten halfway down the hallway, I heard Jason say, "Dude, she's hot."

"Seriously," Logan said. "Shut up."

The butterflies in my stomach went crazy. Then Jason called out, "Bye, Flora!" and I waved, without looking back.

Chapter 20
Sauerkraut and Eggs

The Academy atrium was packed with kids and staff members when I got there. I threw my backpack into one of the wooden cubbyholes that lined the walls outside the dining hall, stepped over a couple of bags of tennis rackets to get to the biometric hand screen, and punched in my code.

I stepped into the big, airy room and my stomach did flip-flops. All I saw were groups of kids laughing, talking, and having a great time. Why hadn't I gone back to the dorm to look for Samantha first? I scanned the room for friendly faces while I walked toward the juice bar. Nikesha's table, near the windows, was full. Sperry was sitting with some of the coaches. Samantha was nowhere in sight. Logan waved hello from a corner booth that was chock-full of boys. "We've got plenty of room," he said and nudged Jason up against the wall.

I wasn't keen to sit on some pole-vaulter's lap, so I said, "I'm cool."

But I wasn't. Somewhere between the door and the juice bar I'd lost my appetite. And to make matters even worse, the

Queen Bs were sitting just off to my right. "Maybe she's considering a juice fast," Kaylee said.

Zoe briefly caught my eye and then looked away. I seriously wondered what Zoe was doing hanging out with those two girls. I watched Kaylee raise her glass to me in a mock toast. "Farm girl's gonna need more than that."

Tatiana didn't have to look up from inspecting her ponytail for split ends to know who Kaylee was talking about. "I'd suggest liposuction and the first flight back to Maine." This cracked them up. I froze, too embarrassed to turn around and let them see my bright red cheeks.

When the man behind the juice bar asked for my order a second time, I forced myself to speak. "I'll have a strawberry banana smoothie with protein powder, please." While I waited for the blender to mix my ingredients, I figured out a way to get from the juice bar to the hot food line without walking back past the Queen Bs. Then I grabbed my smoothie, squeezed behind a table of ice hockey players from Sweden, took a tray, and slowly worked my way down the hot food line. I found myself reading the nutrition cards placed in front of each hot dish, over and over. MASHED POTATOES 1 SERVING = 237 CALORIES, 4 GRAMS PROTEIN, 35 GRAMS CARBOHYDRATE, 9 GRAMS FAT

At that point, I didn't care what I had for dinner, so I took a spoonful of this and a spoonful of that until my plate was full. I grabbed some bottled water and turned back toward the main room and its bustling booths and tables. I hoped, prayed, there would be an open seat at a table of someone I recognized, but there wasn't.

When I'd settled in at a corner table on the edge of the room I looked at my plate—lasagna, sauerkraut, and scrambled eggs. Yuck. At least I had the smoothie. I tried to project some Sperry-like confidence as I sucked the smoothie up through a straw. I told myself, I'm perfectly comfortable sitting alone in the dining hall. All alone. In fact, I prefer it. But who was I kidding? Back home this never would have happened to me.

I leaned back and studied the massive chandelier overhead. Everyone loved the chandelier. I know what Mémère would have called it—a monstrosity—but I thought it was the most beautiful thing I'd ever seen, a true work of art. It was made from actual sports gear: tennis rackets, figure skates, hockey sticks, skis and poles, basketball nets, a rowing oar, a kayak paddle, a bicycle wheel, and soccer boots. They were all stuck together into one big glob, and lights poked out from the insides of figure skates and the ends of ski poles. It was crazy, but it worked. It was the perfect sculpture for a sports academy.

I felt a tap on my shoulder. *Zoe!* "Hey, Zoe," I said.

"I'm sorry about them," she said, quickly glancing over her shoulder.

I looked around all paranoid, like maybe Tatiana and Kaylee had put Zoe up to this conversation, as a joke or something. "Whatever," I muttered.

"I know they can be a little mean—"

"A little?" I rolled my eyes.

She seemed embarrassed. "They're really good players." I looked down at my plate, started eating again. "It's just," Zoe said, "I play with them back home, and I don't really know anyone else here."

"And your point is?"

She looked over her shoulder again. "I just wanted to say, sorry."

Part of me didn't care about the Queen Bs and their drama, but another part of me felt sorry for Zoe. "If you ever want to hang out, I'm here."

"Okay," she said. "Thanks."

I watched Zoe walk away and wondered, *What was that all about?* If the Queen Bs were playing a game, I didn't know the rules. And honestly, I couldn't be bothered to learn them.

Be my friend, don't be my friend. I'm here for two weeks—with one goal—to make Matt's U-15 team.

Chapter 21
Different Gravy

The next morning, the second full day of camp, we awoke to gray skies, cooler temperatures, and a light rain. Some of the players from warmer climates complained, but not me. It reminded me of Maine. Plus, one of my goals was to wear every piece of team gear at least once during ID Camp, so I was psyched to have an excuse to wear my wet-weather gear.

The rain jacket was on my bed, where I'd laid it out before I went to eat. After breakfast with a super-social Samantha—or the "mayor," as I called her, since she seemed to know *everyone* at the ISA—I slipped the jacket on, rubbed my fingers over the U.S. Soccer patch stitched onto it, and felt a chill run up my spine. I wondered if I'd always have that kind of reaction to national team gear. I hoped so.

Out on the pitch, Rainey climbed up on a bench. "Good morning, all you fabulous U-14s," she said.

We jumped up and down and screamed, "Good morning, Rainey!"

"Oh, yeah, I like this enthusiasm," she said. "Okay, how

many of you start training by sitting on the ground and stretching?" One hundred hands shot up. "Good. Stretching is excellent, but today we're going to teach you a new way to stretch. What we do at the national level is something a bit different—we call it active stretching." She hopped off the bench. "Everybody grab a partner, and we'll get started."

I watched everyone start to pair up, my choices getting fewer and fewer. In Acadia everyone wanted to be *my* partner when we did drills. Just as I was starting to truly feel sorry for myself, I felt a tap on my right shoulder. It was Sperry. "You want to partner up?" she asked.

I hesitated. Not because I didn't like Sperry, but because the girl intimidated me. She was just so sure of herself. "Yeah," I said. "That would be great."

Once we'd teamed up into fifty pairs, Rainey and her assistants gave each of us a ball. We used different parts of our feet to dribble the ball, then after a minute or so, Rainey blew her whistle, and we stopped to stretch our ankles. She blew the whistle again and we dribbled for a while, then stopped and stretched our calves. This went on and on as we dribbled and worked our way up the body, from ankles to shoulders. "Just start easy," Rainey said. "You don't want to pull anything. On a day like this, your muscles are cold, so you've got to ease them into moving."

After we'd finished the final dribble-stretch, Rainey told us to pair back up. We watched Rainey and her assistants demonstrate some stretches. Sperry and I faced each other and placed our hands on each other's shoulders. We alternated, gently swinging our legs backward and forward and from side to side. Then we sat on the ground, pressed our feet together to form a diamond with our legs, and slowly pulled each other around in circles. We giggled as our bodies slowly went 'round and 'round. "It's sort of like dancing," Sperry said.

I pulled on her arms so her upper body dropped toward the wet grass. "And this is what I like to call the chest dip."

Sperry looked down at the water marks on her jacket and laughed. "We make a good team."

"A good, wet team," I said as she made me perform the chest dip.

After we'd stretched each other on the ground and standing up, Rainey said, "Now we're going to move on to some running warm-ups." She held up a soccer ball. "This is your friend. Everything we do at the national level is related to . . ."

She threw it in the air, and we all yelled, "The ball!"

"So if you're going to run laps of the field, you're going to do it while dribbling . . ."

"The ball," we said.

Everyone grabbed a ball and slowly started to circle the slippery field.

"Let's share one," Sperry said. We jogged side by side moving the ball between us.

When we passed by Rainey, she said, "I like your initiative, girls."

I jogged backward for a moment. "Individuals don't win international level games." Rainey smiled at us.

Then Sperry looked over her shoulder and said, "Groups do!" We doubled over in laughter as we moved down the touchline.

The warm-up continued with a series of passing exercises. Sperry and I stood several meters apart and used different surfaces of our feet to chip, bend, and pass the ball. We started out close together and gradually moved farther apart. Balls sprayed all over the pitch as everyone tried to do more and more fancy things with the ball.

After a bit, the coaches divided us into eight teams. Sperry and Nikesha were on my team, Team B. But so were the Queen Bs. All three of them. Nikesha caught me frowning at the trio from California. "I know," she said quietly to me. "But we could all end up on a national team together. So we've got to make the effort. They're good soccer players."

"They are," I admitted, having observed them yesterday.

"Maybe we can teach them to channel that meanness toward our opponents," Sperry said. And then she screwed up her face, as if to say, *Maybe not*.

I pulled my ponytail tighter and laughed. "Okay, okay. I'll do like my Mémère says and kill 'em with kindness."

The seventeen of us on Team B were assigned to one of the far fields. We trudged through the wet grass, led by Tatiana. The coaches organized us into two groups of keepaway, but this wasn't like any game of keepaway I'd played in Maine. Six or so girls formed a circle, with two more in the middle. The ones in the circle tried to maintain possession of the ball and keep it away from the girls in the middle. Once we got good at the drill, they added a second ball. We took the drill seriously, but we also found time to learn each other's names and giggle and bond. I loved this drill, and I was good at it, but I also knew I wouldn't be doing it back home because the kids in Acadia didn't have the ball skills to do it properly.

During a water break, I stood behind Tatiana and Kaylee at the water jug while they complained loudly enough for everyone to hear.

"When are we going to get to play?"

"I know. I'm so sick of drills."

"They can't figure out who's the best if they don't watch us play an actual game."

I saw Laura, a tall, moon-faced assistant coach, remove a pen from her back pocket and make a note on her clipboard. I took a few bites of a nutrition bar and a swig of water and jogged back onto the pitch. The coaches were watching our every move.

They had us play lots of short 3 v. 3 games as they switched around the combination of players. Before long, I'd learned everyone's name—*thanks, Mémère!*—and finally started to feel like I fit in. Like I belonged here. We took another water break and then went back out for a series of 1 v. 1 contests with small goals. They called it "flying changes." I called it wicked fun, especially when I went up against Kaylee (goal for me), Zoe (goal for me), and Tatiana (no goal for you).

Toward the end of training, we spent some time working on corners and free kicks. In Acadia, I took every corner and free kick, but at ID Camp I realized pretty quickly that I was good but not good enough to take corners and free kicks at the national level. I nailed a few awesome ones, but not nearly as many as, say, Sperry. Just before I took one free kick, I noticed Matt had arrived at our field. I waited to make sure he was watching, stepped up, and drove the ball from the edge of the area right over the keeper's hands into the upper 90. *Sweet.* I glanced at Matt. He scrunched up his face like he'd smelled cow poop, scribbled something on his clipboard, and walked away.

I wanted to scream, *Dude, are you blind?* Instead I picked up another ball, smacked it down on the ground, stepped back, and drilled it into the net.

⚽ ⚽ ⚽

Later, when I was putting on my sweats, I overheard a few girls talking about Matt, how he had a daughter our age, but hardly ever saw her since his divorce. No matter how much I didn't like Matt, he *was* the U-15 coach, and it seemed mean—and reckless—to talk about him behind his back. So I walked away and joined a different group of girls that were being entertained by Nikesha, who was acting out all the parts of some crazy story about riding on the New York City subway at night.

A little bit later, just before we broke for lunch, Matt gathered all the girls back at the main field. He strutted around in front of us and pretended to tug on an imaginary pair of suspenders. "Will you look at those uniforms," he said. "That's different gravy."

Everyone laughed. "You got me," Rainey said to him. "What the heck is different gravy?"

"Ah, you bloody Americans. Your understanding of the English language, it's shocking." Matt paused for full dramatic effect and then said, "Different gravy means they're pretty special." That was the first time we'd seen Matt laugh at himself.

"Right, then," he said. "Back to business. What are the four things you can control in football?" No one answered. It looked like the other girls were as scared of Matt as I was. "Well, I'll tell you what you can control. Your effort, your enthusiasm, your sportsmanship, and your skills." Matt let his words sink in.

"So what can't you control?" Again, no takers. "How about," he said, "the score, the referee, your coach's decisions, other people's expectations, your opponents' ability, the weather and pitch conditions?"

He jumped down off the bench and paced in front of us. "Girls, we've only got two weeks for this camp. Don't waste your time worrying about what you can't change. Just go out there and get the job done. To quote Yoda, 'Do or do not. There is no try.'"

I smiled. Wait till Rémi heard that the U-15 Girls' National Team coach was a Jedi Master fan who quoted lines from *Star Wars*.

Every little bit I learned about Matt helped. I thought to myself, *Before this camp is over I'm gonna crack you, Matt Keene. And then you're gonna pick me for your team.*

Chapter 22
Speaking of Boys

One of my new favorite things in life was rest period. We didn't have those back on the farm. But at the ISA, rest period—or afternoon napping—was mandatory. The idea was to get us off our feet, so our bodies could rest and recover from morning training and be fresh for afternoon or evening training.

There were no TVs in the dorm rooms, and the Internet was off-limits, except for doing homework projects, so most kids spent rest period sleeping, reading, or doing homework. Since I wasn't missing school, I decided to lie on my bed and relax. I moved my pillow to the middle of the bed, scooted my butt toward the headboard, and raised my legs up against the wall. This was how Samantha found me when she entered the room.

"Ooooh. That feels so good, doesn't it?" she said.

"Yeah, my legs are a little wobbly after this morning's training."

Samantha dropped her bag on the floor, changed into shorts and a T-shirt, and climbed under her covers. We both had large bottles of water on the floor next to our beds. Samantha jumped out of bed and pulled the blinds down on the window. "Better," she said and climbed back under the covers. "I met my future husband today."

"What?" I laughed.

"His name's Luc, he's French Canadian, from Montréal, gorgeous, tall, chocolately brown eyes, and he's an ice hockey player." Samantha rolled onto her back and shook her arms and legs in the air. "Did I mention he has no idea I exist?"

"But he's okay with the whole wedding thing?" I asked.

"Not exactly," Samantha said. "Truth?" I nodded. "I was getting an ultrasound on my ankle from Tony, and Luc was talking to him about doing a physical therapy internship. He's had a lot of injuries and can't play hockey right now, so he's thinking about going to college to become a sports trainer."

"College?"

"Oh, yeah, did I mention he's older than me?"

"Like college old?"

"He looks young." Samantha laughed. "Maybe he skipped a few grades."

"Speaking of boys," I said, not sure if I really wanted to go there with Samantha. But once she'd propped herself up on one arm, and motioned with the other to get on with the story, I didn't really have a choice. "Do you know Logan Livingston?"

"I love him."

Crap. "Really?" I said, all casual.

"Well, not *love* him, love him." *I'm listening.* "I've known him forever. We went to the same gym when I lived in Boston. He used to be a gymnast, but then he got too tall and switched to pole vaulting."

Samantha went on and on about how gymnasts make good pole-vaulters because of their strength, coordination, timing, and attention to technique, but all I could focus on was that she didn't *love* him, love him. Not that *I* loved Logan, but I *liked* him.

"Wait," she said. "How do you know Logan?"

I told her about meeting him at the airport and that we'd bumped into each other a few times yesterday. I left out the part about him rubbing his thumb against my pinkie—that sounded so lame, after the fact—and that he gave me constant butterflies.

"You like him." I blushed. Nodded. I half expected Samantha to make fun of me, but she seemed genuinely happy. "Logan's super-nice. Do you want me to find out if he likes you—"

"No! Don't do that!" I didn't need Samantha meddling. I might be new to the boy thing, but I was doing perfectly fine on my own, thank you very much.

"Okay," she said. "But we should all hang out."

"Yeah," I said, and we both went quiet for bit.

"So how are things with Matt?" Samantha asked. "Is he still a . . . what do you call him?"

"A wackadoodle," I said. "Yes. He is."

Samantha took a sip from her bottle. "Why do you think he bugs you so much?"

"It's not like he's mean—"

"He's just not nice."

"Exactly. I wish he were more like Rainey. I'm not afraid to talk to her about stuff. Kind of like with my coach back home, Coach Roy."

"What's he like?"

"He's like the way I wish my dad was." My eyes flew open, and I covered my face with my hands. "I can't believe I just said that. That's terrible."

"Sounds like it's kind of true." Samantha cracked her knuckles. One at a time. "Can't change how you feel."

"Since my mom died . . . it's been hard. She loved soccer. Loved that I played soccer. But my dad . . . It's complicated—"

"Tell me about it," Samantha said. "The General—my dad—he and I don't get along."

"For me, it's not that my dad and I don't get along. It's just . . ." I wasn't sure I wanted to get into it right then. "He's pretty busy with the farm and stuff."

"If your mom were alive, what do you think she'd say to you?"

"Follow your dream." I closed my eyes. Smiled. "It might sound strange, but Ma's up there, looking down—"

"I know exactly what you mean. My big brother, he died when I was five—it was a horrible accident, I'll tell you about it someday—but anyway, I definitely feel like he's watching me." Samantha took a breath and rolled toward the wall. "I talk to him all the time. I kind of feel like I'm doing this whole gymnastics thing with him."

"I'm sorry. About your brother."

We lay in silence for a few minutes, lost in our thoughts.

"So, I overheard some of the girls talking about Matt today. They said his wife divorced him, took their daughter, and he barely sees her anymore," I said.

"Well, that might explain why he's so . . . the way he is."

"Yeah—" I said, feeling guilty talking this way about Matt.

"He doesn't want to be your friend, he always says things to push you away—he's protecting himself." Samantha laughed.

"I sound like a psychologist! I am officially my mother."

"Your mom's a psychologist?"

"Yup, Mom's a shrink." Samantha rolled her eyes, as if to say, *Don't get me started.* "So what else did they say?"

"The daughter used to be some hotshot soccer star in England. A future female Beckham."

"Used to be?" Samantha said.

"Yeah, apparently his wife——"

"Ex."

"Ex-wife won't let her play soccer anymore. Something about soccer destroying their family," I said.

"He coached Man U, right?" I nodded. "It must have been all soccer, all the time in that household." Samantha tossed her water bottle in the air a couple of times. "How old's the daughter?"

"My age, I think."

"And he decided to coach girls the same age?" Samantha placed the bottle on the floor next to her flip-flops. "Talk about working through your issues. No wonder he's depressed."

"I think my dad's depressed," I said, realizing as I said it that it was probably true.

"Yeah?"

"Yeah." I definitely wasn't going there. Not now. "But they're just rumors about Matt. I don't know if any of it's true."

"Even if only half of it's true, the way he treats you guys makes sense. Look, I know you're older than me and all, but I've been at this national level stuff for a while. All you can do is go out there and play your best at this camp. Matt's never going to be your friend," Samantha said. "Look to Rainey for support——"

"And warm fuzzies."

"Yeah, and try not to let Matt upset you. It's not personal," Samantha said. "Imagine what it must be like to basically lose your daughter . . . and then have a job coaching girls the same age."

"I never thought of it that way."

We stared at the ceiling. After a bit, Samantha said she had to listen to her hypnosis recording. "I do it every day for an hour. It's just as important as all the work I do in the gym. Don't ask me how it works, but it does. It's spooky," she said dragging out the oo's. "I just feel so much more confident afterward."

We sipped from our water bottles.

"I always thought of myself as a mentally strong gymnast, but since I've been listening to this recording, it's like I make better decisions in the gym. I hardly ever question whether I should throw a trick or not. I'm more decisive. And in gymnastics that's the difference between pulling off a move and crashing to the mat."

"I wonder if they make recordings like that for soccer?" I said.

"Of course. They make them for every sport," Samantha said. "You should talk to Charley."

I remembered Matt introduced Charley at our first training session. She had hair just like mine except hers was a beautiful deep, shiny red. Matt called it ginger. "She's one of the Academy sports psychologists, right?" I said.

"Mm hmm. You'd really like her." Samantha adjusted her headphones. "I'm out of here," she said. "See ya on the flip side."

"Later, gator." I quietly swung my legs around and slid under the blankets. I thought about what Matt had said at our first meeting. *Are you willing to do* anything *to make the U.S. team?*

Yes, I am, I thought, as I fell off to sleep. *I'll do hypnosis. I'll do whatever it takes.*

Chapter 23
Lose the Jewels

When we crested the hill behind the gymnasium after rest period and saw that balls had been scattered everywhere on the pitch, we ran screaming down the hill like there was an unlocked candy shop at the bottom. When I got my hands on a ball, I looked around at all the glowing faces, and I knew—I just *knew*—these were my people.

In Acadia, my "obsession," as my friends called it, gave me freak status. Good freak, but still freak. At ID Camp I was surrounded by a hundred girls and a dozen coaches that lived, breathed, and slept soccer. There had to be a word to describe this moment. *Think. Think.* I balanced my ball on the top of my foot, then flicked it up and caught it on the back of my neck. And the word came to me:

Nirvana.

Thank you very much, Mrs. Vanderlip. I'll never complain about another one of your vocabulary pop-quizzes again.

After warm-ups, the coaches announced we'd be playing Team A, 11 v. 11. Since there were seventeen girls on each team, the coaches promised that everyone would get plenty of playing time. And just my luck, I started out on the bench. Laura came over and talked to the six of us benchwarmers. "Relax, you guys," she said. "This doesn't mean anything."

"Of course it doesn't," Nikesha said. "You're saving the best for last, right?"

"Yeah, something like that," Laura said.

Before long, they subbed us all in. I got sent to the front line, which was perfect, since that's where I played in Acadia. I hustled in the other team's final third to help finish the attack and score, but I also dropped back and helped my mid-fielders when they needed it. It felt so good to play 11 v. 11. The Queen Bs were right; games were way more fun than drills and stretching. I flubbed a couple of shots on goal—one went wide, the other high—but otherwise I held my own. The most exciting thing was the level of play; it made Acadia Central look like kiddie soccer.

The coaches pretty much just let us play. They huddled together on the touchline, talked quietly, and made notes on their clipboards. Toward the end of the first half, I started to feel tired. I wasn't used to the faster pace and more aggressive style of play. At one point, I slowed to a walk, stopped, and put my hands on my thighs to catch my breath. "Pick it up, Flora," Matt said. "Pick it up." My already flushed cheeks turned a brighter shade of red.

Tatiana bumped me as she jogged by. "Pickup? No, I'd say you're more of a dump truck." Some of the other girls heard her. None of the coaches did.

It took everything I had not to scream, *Shut your whiny pie hole, Tatiana. He wasn't talking to you.*

⚽ ⚽ ⚽

At the half, Matt called both teams together. "When you play with just two forwards, you've got to work hard to get the ball up to them. And as for those two up front, you've got to be quick. Team B, Kaylee, I like your hustle, but Flora, you're moving like a truck in first gear. You need to get the lead out." I couldn't believe he singled me out like that. "All right, jog on, second half." Matt signaled to me. *Now what?*

"Yes," I said.

He motioned to his throat. "Lose the jewels, Princess."

"Pardon me?"

"This isn't a fashion show—"

"But—"

"Lose. The. Jewels." I couldn't remove the necklace. I couldn't. "Crack on." He was getting impatient.

Rainey came over and stood between us. "Easy, Matt, it's just a necklace."

The look in my eyes must have said, *It's not just a necklace.* Rainey leaned in close, so only I could hear. "It's special, huh?" I nodded and tried to hold back the tears. "Okay, I'm gonna unclasp it—"

I took in a sharp breath and said, "Itsmymoms."

"I'll be careful," she said. "It's just a rule. You can't wear a necklace." Rainey slid the soccer ball charm off the chain, reached into her pocket, and pulled out a small safety pin. "How about during training you pin the charm,"—she reached inside the collar of my jersey—"to your sports bra? That way you'll have it with you." I dipped my head once. Rainey pinned the charm by its little silver loop to my bra. She pulled my jersey back over it, rested her hand on the hidden silver ball, and said, "Our little secret."

She showed me the chain and pointed to her pocket.

I nodded. *"Merci."*

"Crack on, Flora," Matt called from farther down the touchline.

I ran onto the pitch and hustled for every ball. The thought of playing without the soccer ball charm had shaken me. My breathing was labored as I tried to settle myself back down. Sperry jogged past. "You okay?"

"I will be," I said.

And I really would have if Tatiana, my *teammate,* hadn't started calling me dump truck again. The coaches were too busy complimenting her play to hear her nasty comments. And if it wasn't enough being abused by the leader of the Queen Bs, Matt seemed to have it in for me, too. It felt like he was punishing me for wearing a necklace to practice.

If I didn't put enough power behind a shot, he'd say, "What have you got—a chocolate leg?" When I flinched going for a header, he said, "You've got a head like a turtle's neck." And when I had trouble controlling a one touch, he said, "Take that trampoline off your foot."

If it had been any other training session, any other camp, I might have been able to laugh. Chocolate leg? Turtle's neck? Was this guy speaking English? But there was too much on the line. I started to wonder if the Queen Bs were right; maybe I didn't belong at ID Camp. I was trying my hardest. Didn't that count for anything in Matt's book?

At one point, Sperry passed me the ball, and I dribbled up the right flank. I was way too far wide to shoot. I should have passed. Zoe was open, so was Sperry. *Dump it. Dump it.* But I didn't. All my anger and frustration with Matt and Tatiana collided, and before I knew it, I'd fired off a stupid shot on goal. Of course it didn't go in. I wanted to plug my ears because I knew what was coming. "Lass, you've got a foot like a sheriff's badge."

I wanted to scream, *Speak English! Or shut up.*

A couple of minutes later, I had the ball; again, I was too far out with the wrong angle. Kaylee yelled, "Flora, square." No chance was I sending it sideways to her. I whaled on the ball. It flew so high over the goal, the keeper didn't move.

Matt blew his whistle.

"I think we've seen enough stuff ups for one day," he said looking straight at me. "Let's try a four-five-one. That's four defenders, five midfielders, and Tatiana, you stay up front. Flora, move to right outside back."

Right outside back? Was he joking? Defense? I'd never played defense. Ever. I was a forward. *A forward*, I wanted to scream. "Come on, Maine-y." I felt Nikesha's arm around my shoulder. "Don't let the turkeys get you down."

"The four-five-one is probably a new formation to most of you," Matt said, but all I could hear was, *Flora, move to right outside back.* "It's a defensive formation, a good way to preserve a lead." *Right outside back?* "But if your two midfield wingers play a more attacking role, it's basically a four-three-three. It's also a good way to control the pace of the game with your defensive midfielders. Let's give it a go, shall we?"

Nikesha and I walked to our backfield. "I just want to punch something."

"It's only day two; you've got twelve more days to show your stuff," she said.

When I didn't say anything, Nikesha stopped in front of me, turned around, and swiveled her hips. I laughed. "Is that how defenders show their stuff?"

"I'm from New York, baby. We do things differently," she

said. "Hey, girl, you're doing amazing. Soccer's not all about offense—"

"But I've never played defense," I said in a tone so whiny I surprised myself.

"So learn." I didn't want to play right outside back. I wanted to play where I was comfortable, on the front line. Nikesha rested her hands on my shoulders. "Trust me," she said. "It's fun back here."

And then I realized what a jerk I was being. Nikesha. Cool Nikesha. Everyone-wants-to-be-her-friend Nikesha was begging me to be on her "team." *You want friends? Get over yourself.* I smiled. "Maybe I won't have to run as much back here."

"I like you, Maine-y. Have from the minute you almost barfed your eggs on me."

Chapter 24
Apology Not Accepted

After the game, Nikesha and I walked toward the dorms together. When we passed the coaches' offices, I turned to her and said, "I gotta do something. I'll swing by your room later."

"Okay, I'll wait for you, and we'll go to dinner," Nikesha said.

I couldn't explain it, but I just had to see Matt. When I arrived at his office, the door was open, and he was working at his computer. I tapped lightly on the doorframe. He didn't react. I didn't know what to do next, so I just stood there. After several moments, Matt spoke without looking up from his computer. "You're going to have to try harder than that to get my attention, Miss Dupre."

That wackadoodle. He knew I was standing there the whole time.

"I'm sorry—"

"I don't want to hear apologies," he said and slowly spun his chair in my direction.

I walked into the office and tried again. "I just wanted to

say I'm sorry if I disappointed you today."

"It's not me you should be worried about disappointing. I'm not trying to make a national team. You are." He kept talking, but I found myself distracted by a photo pinned to the bulletin board just over his right shoulder. It had to be Matt and his family. They were at the beach. The wind was blowing his daughter's blonde hair around. The three of them had their arms around each other and were laughing. They looked ridiculously happy. "I asked, are you pleased with how you played today?"

I hadn't been listening, but I knew I had to say something, so I blurted out the first thing that came to mind. "Happy? I mean, I was happy with how I hustled in the first half." He seemed interested in what I had to say, so I went on. "I was surprised by the pace of the game. I'm not used to that. And I'm not used to playing with such good players."

"What about all those shots on goal?" Matt leaned back in his chair and put his feet up on his desk. "That was shocking."

I screwed up my face. "Yeah, those. No, I'm not so proud of those." I took a moment to figure out what to say next. "I was just . . . frustrated."

"Yeah, well, welcome to the big leagues. You're not in Kansas anymore—"

"Maine."

He looked down at his desk and started to rearrange the piles of paper. "Anything else?"

I wanted to ask him about the photo. About his daughter. "I wanted to say I'm sorry—"

"What did I say about apologies?" Matt put his feet back on the floor.

"Wait." I raised my hand. "Let me finish. I'm sorry I

disappointed myself today, and I'm not going to do that tomorrow."

"If you say so." Clearly getting a nice word from this man was next to impossible.

"Okay," I said. "I'll see you later." I reached for the door to pull it closed behind me.

"You can leave it open—"

The door clicked shut. I smiled.

Wackadoodle.

Chapter 25
Type A Bloody Overachievers

That evening the entire camp gathered in the auditorium for what Rainey predicted would be a very special evening. I'd spent dinner with Nikesha, Sperry, Hanna, and a couple of other girls and was happy to have people to hang out with. I'd told them all my nickname for the trio from California. As we were waiting for the evening program to begin, we watched Tatiana and Kaylee position themselves dead center in the auditorium. A few minutes later, Zoe walked into the room, headed toward our group—*finally she's wised up*, I thought—but when she made eye contact with Tatiana and saw the empty seat they'd saved for her, she changed direction. She gave a little wave to Nikesha before sitting down. "Poor Zoe," Nikesha said. "Sucked into the beehive once again."

"Yeah, Zoe seems nice," said Sperry.

"She is," Hanna added. "I think she feels pressure to hang out with those two because they know each other from ODP."

"She seems uncomfortable being lumped into the Queen Bs," Sperry said.

"Wouldn't you?" Nikesha asked.

"Now, now girls," I said. "Play nice . . . or I'll put you in my dump truck and drive you right back to your rooms."

"That's my girl." Nikesha elbowed me. "Making lemonade out of lemons. I like you, Maine-y." She turned to Sperry. "We've got us another confident one to add to our group."

Our group? I was part of their group? "Thanks." I played it all cool, but on the inside I was screaming, *Yes, yes, yes!*

The lights in the room dimmed, and everyone hustled to find a seat. Rainey hopped up on the floodlit stage. "I want to start tonight by addressing something that's been bothering me," she said. "Many of you girls have asked us what's next, what team you're going to make now that you're here." She looked out over a sea of nodding heads. "Here's the thing: you made this camp."

A couple of girls rolled their eyes. One even groaned out loud. Rainey kept going. "I know you think we're lying to you, but that's the truth. There is no making a team. Sure, Matt's here trying to put together the U-15 team, but these two weeks are about giving you girls a taste of what playing at the national level is like. We want you to have fun, get to know each other, see if this is something you want to do in the future."

Matt stepped up. "May I?"

"Absolutely."

"I don't know what it is with you bloody Americans." Leave it to Matt to cut right to the point. "You're such bloody over-achievers. You never take time to enjoy your success. You're always moving toward the next thing."

Rainey smiled.

"Back in England we spend a lot of time drinking tea,"

Matt said. "It's a big part of our culture. We sit, we stop, we reflect, we enjoy. I'd like you girls to put your little Type A personalities on hold, if just for the amount of time it takes to drink a 'cuppa, and enjoy. Celebrate the fact that you're here."

He stepped aside and waved Rainey forward. "Matt's right," she said. "It's a huge deal that you're here. Do you know how many thirteen- and fourteen-year-old girls wish they could be here right now? U-14 Girls' National Team ID Camp is merely the beginning; this won't be your only chance to try out for a national team. It's simply the first step."

Matt stepped back up to the microphone. "My job for the next twelve days is to identify girls for the U-15 team. But you need to know that that is a fluid process. I'm not going to name a complete team at the end of this camp. I'm going to have a good sense of who will play for the U-15s, but I'm also going to have an extensive list of maybes."

Matt took a long look at the one hundred girls assembled before him.

"If you're not selected for the U-15s, it doesn't mean you'll never play for a national team. Things change, skills improve, bodies grow. There are plenty of girls on the current Women's National Team who failed to make the U-15s, U-16s, and so on."

Rainey said, "More than anything we want you to enjoy yourselves. Listen, learn, and go home and work on what we've taught you here."

Just then, the side door of the auditorium opened and a big, strong woman with shoulder length blonde hair walked into the darkened theater. "I see our special guest has arrived," Rainey said.

We couldn't believe it. Cat Whitehill, a defender on the

U.S. Women's National Team, was in the same room as us. Nikesha, Sperry, and I instinctively reached for each other's hands.

Cat jumped up on the stage and spoke to us for nearly an hour. She talked about playing college soccer at the University of North Carolina, and she answered questions about what we could expect if we made a national team. She told us about the good (travel, winning), the bad (travel, losing), and the ugly (injuries) of being an elite soccer player.

"The most important thing," she said, "is to keep working hard and keep having fun." And then Cat said something that hit me in the chest. "Physically, you either have it or you don't. If you have a bad practice, you can make up for that, but you need to stay consistent with your confidence; that's something that will help take you to the next level." I felt my new friends' elbows nudge my own.

Toward the end of the evening, someone asked Cat for her autograph. "I'm not going to sign any autographs," she said.

Some of the girls said, "No!" Everyone was surprised.

"Let me finish," Cat said. "I don't want to sign autographs because I want you to think of me as your friend, your mentor. I don't want to be some high and mighty national team player. You girls are part of the National Team program, and so am I. We're just at different ends of the spectrum. In a sense, we're teammates. So no autographs . . . but let's take some photos."

Back in my room I typed an e-mail to Coach Roy:

Subject: Guess who's taller than Cat Whitehill?
How do I know this? Because I met Cat Whitehill tonight!!!!
Jealous, much? She's awesome. Big, strong. Actually

everyone was saying I look like her. Except her thighs are like fifty times bigger than mine!

She said something tonight that really made me think . . . 'physically, you either have it or you don't' . . . Let me tell you, Coach Roy, if that's what national team players look like, I have it!

I smiled knowing how happy Coach would be when he heard I'd met Cat. Thinking of Coach Roy reminded me of just how important ID Camp was for me. All the other girls had club teams and ODP to fall back on if they didn't make the U-15s. But in Acadia I didn't have any of that. All I had was three months of high school soccer per year. And now that I'd been here, played with the best girls my age in the country, I knew I needed more of a challenge than high school soccer if I wanted to reach my goal of playing for the U.S.A. in the Olympics and the World Cup.

I didn't care what Matt and Rainey said tonight. I *had* to make the U-15s. ID Camp was my only chance to get into the National Team system. If I didn't make the U-15s, I'd go back to Maine and probably never get another chance to play in front of national team coaches. They definitely weren't coming to Acadia for our rematch with Aroostook. ID Camp was my one and only shot at a national team.

And I knew one other thing for certain. There was no way I wanted to be on Matt's long list of maybes. Not after I met Cat Whitehill.

Chapter 26
Eat, Sleep, Play

The next six days passed by in a crazy, busy blur. We went from breakfast to morning training to lunch to rest period to afternoon games to dinner and finally to sleep. I was so immersed in ID Camp that I didn't give much thought to the harvest going on back home. And whenever I called the farmhouse, everyone seemed more interested in hearing about what I was doing than talking about picking potatoes.

As for camp, I'd never played so much soccer in my life, which I loved, but my legs were feeling it, especially my hamstrings, which were stiff and sore. Samantha was great about helping me stretch them during rest period and in the evenings. On the boy front, Logan and I ran into each other several times a day—something I hoped was both our doing. And Nikesha, Sperry, and I had become besties, plus I'd met a ton of people who were permanent residents at the ISA so I never worried anymore about having to sit alone in the dining hall. Of course, it helped having the mayor of the ISA as my roomie.

Probably the hardest part for everyone at ID Camp—myself included—was playing positions we'd never played before. Back home, most of us played attacking positions on the front line or in the midfield. But at ID Camp the coaches constantly swapped our positions around so everyone spent some time each day as a forward, midfielder, and defender. The only girls exempt from the coaches' chess game were the goalies.

Today, Sperry and I were discussing this as we stretched each other out before training. "I feel like I'm going crazy," I said, rolling onto my back. "Every time I settle into a new position, they move me somewhere else."

Sperry pushed my right leg toward my ear. "Do you trust them?"

"Ow," I grabbed at my right hamstring. "The better question is, do I trust you?"

"Sorry." She eased off. "So, do you? Trust them?"

"Trust." I sat up and took a big bite of banana. "I never thought of it that way."

"Chew," Sperry said.

"Sorry." I swallowed the banana and then some water. "I don't know about trust. I'm just trying to keep my head above water out there." Sperry nodded. "I'm totally stressed about making mistakes. . . ."

Erika, one of the assistant coaches, knelt down between us and cupped her hand around her ear. "Eavesdropping. Bad habit." She shrugged her shoulders and said, "Flora, you can't think like that. You need to take chances, be creative. You won't be able to do that if you're worried about making mistakes." Easy for her to say when it was *my* dream on the line. "Just my two cents," she said and stood up.

"You're right, Erika," I said in my sugary-polite voice. "That's great advice. I'll try it."

When she was out of earshot, Sperry leaned in and said, "Could you hate her any more?"

"She's a total buttinski," I said, and we both cracked up.

I had a sudden urge to hug Sperry, to thank her for seeing the real Flora, the competitive, driven, soccer-loving girl I was. I punched her in the arm and said, "You get me."

Sperry threw a water bottle at me.

When the first practice game started, Sperry and I were assigned to the bench, which gave me time to think about our conversation. Did I trust the coaches? I wanted to, but there was so much on the line. I also thought about how pigheaded I'd been about playing other positions. I don't know what my problem was. A month earlier, before Acadia's season began, but after the Olympic Development Program tryout in Boston, Coach Roy had said he was thinking of making me an attacking midfielder, instead of a forward. He said moving to an attacking midfield position would force me to be more creative. It would turn me from a pure goal scorer into more of a playmaker. He said I needed to do that if I wanted to develop as a player. The plan had been to start me in midfield against Aroostook. I smiled as I thought back to the day of the cancelled Aroostook game.

Sperry tugged on my ponytail. "Why so smiley?"

"I'm just thinking about how fast bad things can turn into good things."

"Ooooh, my little philosopher." We leaned against each other. And to think this girl used to scare me.

"Sperry, Flora, you're in," Rainey said from the other end of the bench. We jogged onto the pitch. Sperry was given the creative role of attacking midfielder. I was right behind her, as a more defensive-minded midfielder. A destroyer, Matt called it. I loved that. Flora Dupre. Destroyer.

Sperry and I quickly led our side on a three-goal rampage. Every time we scored, we did a little dance—not an obnoxious we're-so-great dance, more like a we're-loving-life dance. Part of me—a big part—wished ID Camp would never end and that I didn't have to go home in six days.

At the end of practice, the coaches gathered us around, and Rainey hopped up on a bench. "I'm really proud of how you girls are adapting to different positions. I know it's hard, but we're doing it for a few reasons. One, so we can evaluate your skills; two, so you can appreciate what it's like to play different positions; and three, because we might figure out you're best suited to a position you've never had to play on your club team."

I only half-listened to Rainey as I packed up my gear— I knew what she was saying didn't apply to me. It was obvious I was a forward—okay, maybe an attacking midfielder. But I certainly wasn't a defender. That was Nikesha's thing. I cringed thinking back to the second day of camp when Matt punished me for wearing Ma's charm and made me play right back. *Right back!* Like he was going to use me as anything other than an attacker on the U-15s!

While Rainey talked, we stretched to stay warm. "Don't get all hung up on positions," she said. "Soccer's a fluid game. You play where you're needed. If you're a midfielder, one minute you fall back and play defense; the next, if the opening presents itself, you move into a scoring position."

I looked around at the coaching staff. *I trust you guys*, I thought to myself. *I do. Just don't mess this up for me.*

Rainey zipped her jacket up to her chin. "Everybody head in and get warm," she said. "We'll see you after dinner tonight in the auditorium."

"What's tonight?" Tatiana asked.

Matt turned briefly to smile at the other coaches and then said to us, "You'll see."

"Maybe it's a movie," Zoe said twirling around in a circle.

"Dream on, California," Nikesha said. "It's the first cut."

The moment the words came out of Nikesha's mouth, I felt like I'd been punched in the gut. *First cut?* I'd been concentrating so hard on not screwing up, I'd forgotten all about cuts. The whole way back to the dorms I hung at the back of the group. I couldn't get Nikesha's words out of my head. What if she was right and tonight *was* the first cut? What if *I* was cut?

Chapter 27
U-14 Group of Death

I was glad Samantha was still at training when I got to our room. I took a quick shower and then lay down on top of my covers. I closed my eyes, and the next thing I knew, I was in a half-awake, half-asleep dream world and totally weirded out.

Of course, Matt was in my dream, and like anything involving Matt, it was strange. He was coaching a soccer match in our potato fields in Acadia. The players were running in and out of my relatives, who were acting like it was completely normal to pick potatoes with twenty-two girls weaving around them playing soccer. Mémère and Pépère were operating a concession stand out of the back of the broken-down red pickup. There was a JumboTron scoreboard mounted on top of the barn that read, U-15 GIRLS' NATIONAL TEAM VS THE REIGNING MAINE STATE CHAMPIONS—AROOSTOOK. Tatiana, Kaylee, and Sperry were on the front line for the U.S., decked out in their red, white, and blue gear. Nikesha was the princess of the backfield. The girls from Aroostook were wearing their State Champion jackets over their uniforms. But they weren't last year's jackets—they were *this* year's and they'd been given them because Coach Roy refused to reschedule the game from Harvest Break. The state soccer officials ended the season early on account of Acadia's poor sportsmanship and awarded Aroostook the State Champion.

Every once in a while, Coach Roy would peek out from behind a tree in the woods beyond the team benches, and Robert Landry and his idiot brothers would throw potatoes at him. And then all you could hear were potatoes whacking against trees.

Pa and Uncle Henri were the referees, sprinting up and down the field in black-and-white striped jerseys. Both of them had stretchy gym teacher shorts pulled up *way* over their stomachs. Oh, yeah, and they had big pot bellies and were totally out of breath.

And if all of that wasn't disturbing enough, *I* was the water girl. For *Aroostook*. At one point, Pa ran by and said, "Flora, did you see that Tatiana? She's something else." Before I could say anything Uncle Henri chimed in with, "And she's so polite."

"She's a bitch!" I yelled.

"Dude! Chill." I opened my eyes to Samantha staring at me like I was a crazy person. "Bad dream?" she asked.

I was still half-asleep and completely freaked out, so it took me a few seconds to figure out where I was and what was going on.

"I'm waiting," Samantha said, tapping me on the shoulder with her shampoo bottle.

"What—"

"Who's the bitch?"

"Tatiana."

"Shocking," Samantha deadpanned. "I'll alert the authorities."

I stood up and started to pace in the tiny space between our beds. "There was a soccer game, my dad was the ref, Tatiana and Sperry were friends, the U-15s were playing Aroostook—"

"A-what?" Samantha laughed at me.

"I was the *water* girl!"

"Anxious much?" Samantha said as I sat down on her bed. "Maybe we should call my mom. She could analyze the heck out of this dream."

I didn't need a professional to tell me I was terrified of being cut tonight.

"Can I trust you to be alone long enough to hop in the shower?" Samantha asked. "You're not going to become a complete loony on me, are you?"

I waved her off to the shower like I didn't have a care in the world, but as I listened to the water pound down I realized just how on edge I was about tonight. I hoped Zoe was right and they were going to show a movie—maybe *Gracie*— I loved that movie.

That evening after dinner, the whole camp gathered in the auditorium. All of us girls settled into the plush, red movie theater seats. The coaches sat in wooden folding chairs on the stage.

"Good evening, everyone," Rainey said. "Believe it or not, as of tomorrow we have only five days left of camp."

"Boo," we all yelled.

Rainey motioned for us to quiet down. "With that in mind, we've reassigned the teams."

Suddenly everyone started talking and shifting around in their seats.

"I thought we were watching a movie," Tatiana said.

"We are." Nikesha turned around to look at her. "The movie of your life. Pay attention."

Rainey tapped her finger on the microphone to get us to quiet down. "There will be seven teams," she said. "Teams A, B, C, and D will work with me and Matt. Teams E, F, and G will work with Erika and Laura."

"Told you," Nikesha said a little too loudly into my ear. "It's the first cut." I didn't know if I was more annoyed that it was the first cut or that Nikesha felt the need to point out she'd predicted this was what tonight's meeting was about.

Sperry leaned over and whispered, "Our own U-14 group of death."

Rainey went on to say that while they had identified sixty girls to move on to the U-15 team selection, this didn't mean the girls on Teams E, F, and G should be disappointed.

"Easy for her to say," Nikesha said. Sperry and I nodded in agreement.

"We've posted the team rosters in the hall—"

All one hundred of us raced for the doors of the auditorium.

"I guess we're done here," Rainey said.

Chapter 28
Allez! Allez!

One hundred bloody Type A overachievers pushed and shoved each other to find our names on the seven sheets of white paper taped to the cinderblock wall. My instinct was to flatten every girl standing between me and the rosters—Rainey had told me to embrace my size and strength—but I didn't. Instead, I stood at the back and patiently waited my turn. After making little forward progress, I finally screamed, "Come on, people! *Allez! Allez!*"

The news broke fast and furious. Some girls shrieked, jumped up and down, and hugged each other. Others slunk off down the hall, trying not to bawl in front of the rest of us. As I inched closer to the wall I saw they'd broken down the seven teams, A–G, with one team per page. I couldn't read the names yet—could they have printed them any smaller?

"Hurry up, you silly ninnies," Nikesha said as she used her arms to shove a few screamers out of the way. "Move it."

After what felt like hours, I was close enough to scan the names. I started on the far left with Team A and quickly read down the list. Would it have killed them to put the names in alphabetical order?

I got to the bottom of the page for Team A.

No.

I moved one sheet to the right. Team B. Scanned it.

No.

But Tatiana—*Crap!*—and Kaylee—*Double crap!*—made it.

I took a deep breath. It felt like someone had shoved a fuzzy yellow tennis ball down my throat when I wasn't looking.

Third one's the charm, I heard Mémère's voice in my head. Team C. I read the list. Twice.

My heart started to race.

To my right, I caught Sperry and Nikesha doing the happy dance. *Please, please, please,* I begged the soccer gods.

I moved to the fourth sheet. This time I started at the bottom and scanned my way up.

Nikesha. A few names higher, *Sperry.* I continued to move up the list. *Zoe.* I wasn't sure how I felt about that one.

This is not happening. I *have* to make the U-15s. I can't go back to—

And then I saw it. *Flora Dupre.* The last name. At the top. Team D.

YES!

I sprinted to Sperry and Nikesha like I'd scored a game-winning goal and joined the happy dance. We formed a circle, arms around each other's shoulders, heads leaning toward the center. I was the first to catch my breath. "I don't know if I want to cry or throw up."

Nikesha pointed to a nearby garbage can. "No barfing in the circle of love."

Sperry bear-hugged us. "We did it! And we're gonna make the next cut, too." This set us off into another screaming, dancing frenzy.

We linked arms and skipped Wizard of Oz–style down the hallway. "Ice cream sundae celebration?" Nikesha asked, and we raced each other down the glass passageway toward the dining hall.

As we stood in line for ice cream, I shot off a quick e-mail to Rémi.

Survived the first cut! Yahoooooooo! Nikesha and Sperry are on my team! So is Zoe. I know. ☹ But maybe I was wrong about her. Everyone says she's nice. We'll see. I reserve the right to change my mind!

No sooner had I sent it, then Rémi replied:

You rock! When I called your house with the news they all started screaming and yelling.

And when haven't you reserved the right to change your mind????

Chapter 29
There's No Crying in Soccer

After our ice cream pig-out, I told Nikesha and Sperry I had to go because Samantha was waiting for me back in our room. Actually, Samantha was at a team meeting, but I didn't know how to say to my friends, *Hey, I'm freaking out here and need some time alone to think, so see ya later*. I walked in the direction of Beijing, but once I rounded the corner I slipped my warm-up jacket on and headed toward an exit. When I pushed the door open, the cold mountain air smacked me in the chest. I leaned my head back and blew big, steamy clouds through my lips. I loved the smell, the feel of the raw, cold air in my nose. I inhaled so hard my brain tingled. Maine brain freeze, Ma used to call it.

I passed a few coaches on their way back to their offices, but for the most part the campus was pitch-black and silent. Overhead a beautiful dome of stars blanketed the sky. I kicked off my flip-flops and walked barefoot through the grass. The dew was icy cold between my toes. I stopped at a bench, dried my feet on my pant legs, and then lay back and looked up at the night sky. Sixty girls. I'd made the cut. I couldn't believe it—I mean, I could, but I couldn't. Now I just had to hang in there for five more days. And not get cut.

Lying in the cold night air, I couldn't stop thinking of home. I pulled out my phone, dialed the farmhouse, realized the two-hour time difference—everyone would be asleep— and quickly hit the red hang-up button. *My bad.* I hoped I'd caught it before it rang and woke everyone up.

I missed Coach Roy and his warm fuzzies. I missed Rémi. I missed Mémère and Pépère. And I missed Pa, even if he didn't always seem to understand what soccer meant to me. I even missed picking potatoes. Well, I missed hanging in the fields with my relatives during Harvest Break.

A shooting star streaked across the sky. "Hello, Ma," I said. That's who I really wanted to call—Ma—to tell her I made the cut. I touched the soccer ball dangling from my necklace. A tear ran down my cheek. I wiped it away with the back of my hand, but another one followed, and then I was crying so hard I could barely breathe. I sat up and took big gulps of air.

"What's with the waterworks?" I spun around. *Matt!* What was he doing here? I didn't say anything. "You made the cut," he said, like, *What's your problem?*

"My mother's dead." *Why did I say that?* I wasn't crying about Ma being dead. I was crying because . . . I was just crying.

Matt didn't say anything. "Well, she is," I repeated. Why was I telling him this? I didn't want his sympathy. He didn't need to know about Ma.

"I believe you," he said.

We stared at each other.

Go away.

But he didn't.

"My dad didn't want me to come here." *Flora! Shut up!*

"Is that why you're crying?"

"No. Yes. Maybe. I don't know."

"Well, which is it?"

"I just came out here to be alone . . . you know . . . with my thoughts." *And not with you.*

"And I was just walking back to my office." Matt pointed to the door next to my bench. "To be alone . . . you know . . . with my computer." Matt shrugged his shoulders. "I thought you were waiting for me."

"No," I said. "I just kind of ended up here. Because it was quiet." And then I reminded myself that Matt wasn't the enemy. He was the reason I'd survived the cut. "Actually, I'm— I'm happy, you know . . . relieved, mostly, to make the cut." He didn't say anything. "Thank you," I said so quietly I wasn't sure he heard me, or that I wanted him to.

"Don't thank me yet. You've got five more days to keep impressing me. Oh, and Flora?" He put his key in the lock. "There's no crying in soccer." The light from the room suddenly flooded my bench, and then the office door clicked shut.

"Do I look like I'm playing soccer here?" I said to no one.

Now that I was done crying I couldn't get away from there—and obnoxious, annoying Matt—fast enough. Before I knew it I was opening one of the side doors to the Montréal dorm. Logan's dorm. I could have headed back to Beijing, maybe even gone to the classrooms to see if Samantha's meeting was over, but what can I say? I wanted to see Logan. I don't know how it happened, but somehow over the last week I'd turned into one of those lame stalker girls. It must have been the mountain air. *Yeah, right.* I made a deal with the

Logan-obsessed Flora that we could check for him in Montréal's TV room, but if he wasn't there we were getting the
heck out of his dorm.

But when I peeked in the TV room, there he was, sprawled
out on the couch, clicker in his hand, wearing just shorts and
flip-flops, watching Eric Wynalda and *Fox Football Fone-In*.
He looked so—

"Flora." Logan smiled up at me through half-lidded eyes,
yawned, and ran his hand through his hair. *I want to do that.*
Flora! Get a grip!

He rubbed the sleep out of his eyes, looked at me, and
said, "What's wrong?"

"Nothing—" I croaked.

He sat up. "Have you been crying?"

"Yeah." I tried to downplay it. "Matt," I said and rolled my
eyes. Logan gave me a quizzical look. *Crap!* Now I was going to have to explain. All I'd really wanted to do was catch a
glimpse of Logan and then run back to Beijing with butterflies
in my stomach.

He patted the couch. Muted the TV. I told him about making the first cut, crying in front of Matt—I left out the part
about Ma, too embarrassing—and a white lie about walking
through Montréal looking for Samantha. Logan bought my
white lie and then told me about making his first junior
national team. How nervous he was, how much pressure he'd
put on himself. Looking at him I realized the butterflies were
gone. Yes, Logan was adorable, but he was also an athlete
with a big sugar-coated Olympic dream—just like me. He'd
been there. He understood how important making a national
team was to me.

We stood at the door of the TV room, ready to go to our

separate dorm rooms when Logan said, "Hey, you made the cut." I smiled up at him. He leaned down. *Holy crap! Was he going to kiss me?* "Congrats," he said, and I felt his lips lightly graze my forehead.

How lame was I? My first kiss from a boy was on . . . *the forehead.* But that didn't stop me from running back to Beijing with a smile on my face, like I'd just scored a go-ahead goal against Brazil in the Olympic final.

Chapter 30
Pressure/Cover

I woke up the next morning ready to play soccer. Of course, I wished Matt hadn't seen me crying and that I hadn't told him about my family, but I knew if I wanted to make the U-15s I had to leave all of that behind me. I thought back to what Matt had said last night: *"You've got five more days to keep impressing me."*

Bring it on!

Before official training began, I jogged and dribbled the ball around the pitch. When I passed Matt on the sideline, I tapped him the ball. "Good morning, Matt," I said, all nice and chipper.

He passed it back. "What did you see in the mirror this morning?"

A girl who got kissed on the freakin' forehead. I smiled and said, "A bloody Type A overachiever."

Rainey, who stood a few steps farther down the touchline, called out, "Flora, 1; Matt, 0." I high-fived her as I jogged past. "You're on the board," she said.

We spent the morning working on small-group defending. Matt addressed everyone before we got started. "The point of this morning's training is to show you how to solve problems as a group," he said. "You're used to being the best player on your team and solving problems by yourself." Sixty ponytails nodded in unison. "Welcome to a whole new way of playing. Today we're going to show you how to work together as a group to get the ball from the other team. And then we're going to show you what to do with the ball," Matt said. "But first things first, split up into groups of three."

He said one of us would be the forward and have the ball. The other two would be defenders and have to work together to get the ball away. "This is what we call pressure/cover or second defender tactics," Matt said. "The first defender goes for the ball, and the second defender stands in a position so they can cut off the pass or catch the forward if they dribble past the first defender. Let's go."

Sperry, Nikesha, and I teamed up. I dropped the ball at my feet and toyed with it in front of them. "I don't want to see any hissy fits when you can't get it away from me."

Sperry looked up from tightening her shoelaces and rolled her eyes. "Puh-lease."

We played hard. I was able to keep the ball away from them because they didn't pressure/cover me. They went after me at the same time, and I beat them both. I goaded them and pointed out every missed opportunity. When I was in the middle of one of my taunts, Nikesha slid in from the left and popped the ball away, just far enough for Sperry to pick it up.

"Textbook pressure/cover," Sperry said.

"Beginner's luck," I said.

"Don't you sass me, Maine-y, or you'll be lookin' at a

whole world of hurt," Nikesha said.

"Promises, promises."

We rotated so each of us had a chance to be the forward with the ball. Rainey and Matt watched for a while. They praised our hustle and creativity. Of course, when they were nearby we toned down the trash-talking, but as soon as they were out of earshot we ramped it back up. The morning wore on, and the coaches upped the drill from 2 v. 1, to 3 v. 1, and finally to 5 v. 2. It was such a relief to feel confident again on the pitch. I owned those drills.

During a water break, Matt spoke to the group again. "You see how much easier it is to take the ball away when you've got others to help you. Keep that in mind this afternoon when we play full games. Your instinct is going to be to muscle your way through and solve the problem yourself, because you've been doing it that way for so long. But as you see, it's much easier to defeat someone 2 v. 1 than 1 v. 1. So look around for help. Any questions?"

A girl from Florida, Meagan, called out from the back. "Does the National Team do this?"

"The National Team, the pros, my boys at Man U did it nearly every day," Matt said. "It's like anything, you've got to start small, 2 v. 1. Once you figure that out, you up the pressure a bit, to say 3 v. 2. Ultimately, you get all the way up to a game situation of 11 v. 11."

"What was it like coaching Man U?" another girl in the back, Hanna, asked.

"They were a pack of bloody winghers."

"Winghers?" Kaylee said. "I can't understand a word out of his mouth."

"Join the crowd," Rainey said. "Winghers are complainers."

"Even Beckham?" Sperry asked.

"Don't get me started—" Matt pretended to walk off as we all laughed.

"Ah, come on, Matt, Beckham's an awesome player," Nikesha said.

"You're right about that. One of the best I ever coached," he said. "Enough reminiscing. Let's head in for lunch. Great job out there, girls."

Morning training had been physically hard, but all sixty of us were hyped up as we gathered our stuff. It had been a good session. We'd learned a lot, we'd worked together, and, most of all, we knew we'd made the first cut and were just four and a half days away from making the U-15s.

"Can you believe we're being coached by a guy who coached Manchester United?" Sperry asked.

"I'm waiting for someone to pinch me and tell me this whole U-14 camp is a dream," Nikesha said.

"I was wrong about Matt," I added. "He's a good guy." Nikesha put her hand on my forehead. I pulled away from her. "What are you doing?"

"Checking for a fever." We laughed and then raced each other up the hill.

Chapter 31
Exclamation Points

I decided to drop by the gymnasium where Samantha and the U.S. Junior National Gymnastics Team were training. I figured I'd ask her to join me for lunch if they were about to wrap things up for the morning.

I'd never seen gymnastics before—except on TV—so when I walked into Gymnasium C, I felt like I'd stumbled into a four-ring circus. Tiny, rock-hard girls were working out on the uneven bars, floor, balance beam, and vault. At the far end of the gym, a girl climbed a rope that hung from the rafters, while another practiced flips on a trampoline. Between the floor exercise music, coaches shouting instructions, and feet and bodies banging and smacking on mats and cushions, it was very intense. But it was also really quiet because none of the girls were talking to each other. That seemed so weird to me, especially after spending the morning practicing pressure/cover with my teammates.

I pulled the door closed behind me, dropped my bag on the floor, and leaned against the wall. It took me awhile to find Samantha, and when I did she was sprinting all-out down the vault runway. After she stuck the landing, she waved at me and danced along to the floor exercise music as she crossed the gym to where I sat.

"*Hola chica,*" she said. "*¿Qué pasa?*" I gave her a puzzled look. "It's Spanish. My teammate Galena's teaching me. You like?"

"*Oui, j'aime bien . . . mais pourquoi est-ce que tu apprends l'espagnol plutôt que le français?*

"Is that French?"

"*Oui.*"

"You didn't tell me you speak French."

"So much to learn, Roomie," I said, "so little time."

Samantha lifted my bag and pretended to fall over from the weight of it. "What've you got in there?" Before I could answer, she was on to the next topic. "Hey, how was training this morning?"

"Amazing," I said. "Fantastic. So fun. I'm even convinced Matt might not be—"

"A wackadoodle?"

"Yeah." We both laughed.

A man's voice boomed across the gym. "Sam-uch-ka!"

Samantha scrunched up her face. "Vladimir." I gave her a "who's that?" look. "My super-scary, completely humorless Russian coach," she said. "My Yurchenko awaits."

"Your—what?"

"It's a vault, well, *the* vault. You do a round-off, back handspring—"

"SAM-UCH-KA!"

"Gotta go."

"Okay, I'm gonna eat," I said and started to stand up.

"No!" Sam said. "Wait. Okay? We're almost done. Please?"

"Sure," I said and sat back down.

"Gracias." Samantha did a pirouette, and then danced back across the gym to a very impatient Vlad.

I leaned against the wall and shut my eyes. For a brief moment, I saw my whole experience at the ISA flash through my brain like a SportsCenter highlight reel. Playing with Nikesha and Sperry, flirting with Logan, hanging with Samantha. *It's all good*, I heard the ESPN announcer say.

And it was. I watched Samantha sprint down the runway, do a round-off onto the springboard, a back handspring off the vault, launch herself in the air, spin around two times, and then stick her landing. With her arms raised in the air and Vladimir shouting "Yes!" she winked at me.

It really was. All good.

Half a dozen Yurchenkos later, Samantha packed her gym bag, and we headed outside to sit in the sun before going to the dining hall. As we stretched out on the grass, Samantha placed a plastic bag of ice on her ankle. "You're always icing something," I said.

"Welcome to my world," she said. "I can't remember not being injured."

"I can't imagine always being in pain."

"Injuries aren't always painful. Mostly they're just annoying. You know, nagging stuff." She adjusted the bag. "Like my ankle. I sprained it a while ago, and it's never been the same."

"How'd you sprain it?" I asked.

"On a dismount. Big surprise—that's when most injuries happen. But dismounts are fun. They're like exclamation points to performances. When you stick a dismount it's the best feeling in the world." Samantha laid her head back and looked up at the sky. "My dad hates this sport. Hates the injuries. If it were up to him, I'd quit. Never step foot in a gym again." *Quit? Pa would never make me quit.* "He doesn't get it. Gymnasts are always injured. It's part of the sport. You get really good at ignoring pain."

"That's crazy." I hoped I hadn't offended her, but *seriously* the human body screams in pain for a reason.

"I guess it's hard to understand if you're not a gymnast, but that's just the way it is. With my dad, it's complicated. He's a general, so he's used to everyone doing what he tells them to do. Always being right. Always getting the final say," Samantha said. "I love coming to the ISA for training camps because nobody here bugs me about my injuries."

I couldn't believe how different soccer was from gymnastics.

"Do you think your dad will make you quit?" I asked.

Samantha was silent for a long time. "I don't know. Maybe. He's convinced I'm going to end up with permanent bone damage."

It seemed like he had a point, but I kept silent. Clearly this was a very sensitive issue for Samantha. And who was I to question how she went about pursuing her dream?

"I'll never forgive him if he makes me quit. Never."

"Well," I said. "I hope he doesn't."

"Yeah." Samantha tossed the bag of icy water in a trash can. "For now I've just got to hide my injuries as much as possible. I'm not letting my dad keep me from competing in the Pacific Rim Championships."

Chapter 32
Stupid Soccer Camp

At lunch, Samantha and I sat with her teammate Galena. We spoke in English, French, and Spanish. We had so much fun teaching each other new words and phrases, some more explicit than others. When I looked around the rollicking dining hall, I realized I was one of those kids sitting in a group, laughing, talking, and having a great time. For the first time since I arrived at the Academy, I felt at home. Comfortable. I found myself fantasizing about what it would be like to live and train year-round at the International Sports Academy.

The only downside to the day so far was that I hadn't seen Logan. But I knew if I hung around the dining hall tonight I'd probably see him. For now, I had to get my mind off Logan and onto soccer.

During rest period, Samantha listened to her hypnosis recording while I mulled over my chances of making Matt's U-15 team. I methodically went through all sixty girls and tried to figure out who was national team material. I knew Matt was downplaying the importance of making the U-15s at ID Camp, but he wasn't fooling me. There was nothing left for me back home. I had to make the team. And even though none of the coaches had mentioned it, we all knew that this U-15 team would compete two years from now in the FIFA U-17 Women's World Cup. I wanted to be, *needed* to be, on that roster.

Later that afternoon, we played Team A. I was in my usual place on the front line. We dominated them with the pressure/cover and small-group defending skills we'd learned in morning training. We worked together as units to tackle, slide, and poke the ball away from the players on Team A. Twice Matt called out, "Excellent, Flora," when I cut neatly around my defenders. After the game, Rainey said we looked like a swarm of locusts working together to defeat the enemy.

On the way back to Beijing, I found myself skipping, seriously skipping. Something I hadn't done in, well, at least two years. I reached inside my jersey to touch Ma's soccer charm and smiled. Four days to go, and everything was falling into place.

When I got to our room, I scanned my hand and punched in Rémi's birthday—poor Rémi, I wondered how he was holding up in the fields. As I stepped into the room, I noticed a piece of paper had been slipped under the door.

Dear Flora,
Please come to the Main Office for an important phone message.
Sally

I dropped the note on the desk next to Samantha's laptop. The word important didn't register in my brain, so instead of heading immediately to the Main Office, I took off my grass-stained socks and uniform, lay down for a few minutes on the bed, and replayed our win over Team A. Then I took a long, hot shower, pulled my wet hair up into a chignon—another new skill I'd learned at the Academy, this one thanks to Samantha—and put on some warm clothes before going to the Main Office.

Sally wasn't around, so I showed the note to a crinkly-faced woman behind the desk. "Oh, yes." She puckered her lips and made a sad face. "Sally told me about this."

I'd gotten a bunch of missed calls on my cell from the farmhouse, but I'd ignored them because no one had left a message. It was probably just Mémère wondering where I'd put her favorite muffin pan or some other silly thing. Pépère said she was worse than a teenager when it came to the phone.

Ole prune-face said I needed to call home—right now!—and pointed toward a series of booths that lined one wall of the hallway. I tried not to laugh. Did she seriously want me to use a pay phone? Just to humor her I sat down in an available booth.

But when I pulled out my cell phone I couldn't remember the number to the farmhouse. And the harder I tried, the further it receded into my brain. All I could hear was Tatiana in the next booth rattling on and on to someone back home. I tried to tune her out . . . this was crazy . . . I knew my phone number. . . . It was stored under Home, but it bugged me that I couldn't remember the *actual* number.

And then it came to me. Just to prove a point to myself I punched the numbers into my cell rather than scrolling down to Home. On the second ring, the call connected.

"*Allô?*" Rémi? What was he doing answering our phone at

this time of night? Shouldn't he be at his house? And where was the phone queen, Mémère?

"*Bonsoir*, Rémi. *C'est* Flora. *Ça va?*" For the next several minutes I simply listened. Rémi was sobbing. Between hic-cupy breaths he told me that earlier that afternoon Pépère had suffered a stroke. He was in the barn trying to move some barrels of potatoes. He was alone when he collapsed. No one knew how long he lay on the floor of the barn. Rémi's dad, my Uncle Al, found Pépère, called 9-1-1, and stayed with him until the ambulance took him to County General. Just the men-tion of that place turned my stomach. I hadn't been to County General since Ma died.

I heard Rémi perfectly fine, but in my brain he sounded far, far away. I was thinking about Ma. About that day she died. How afterward, when we went outside to the parking lot, the hugest rainbow I'd ever seen appeared in the sky. Tatiana's voice cut through my thoughts. "Oh, definitely. Kaylee and me are gonna be front line on the U-15s. For sure." *Did that girl ever shut up?* "No, Zoe's been sort of snotty. Acting like she's too good for us."

"Flora? Flora?" It was Rémi. "Are you still there? Are you okay?"

"Yeah, I'm just kind of in shock." It seemed like the right thing to say, but really I was thinking about Ma. And maybe a little about soccer. *Did she just say, "Kaylee and me are gonna be front line on the U-15s"?*

"Flora?"

No way were they going to be on the front line of the U-15s, not if I had anything to do with it.

"So do you want Coach Roy to pick you up at the airport?"

"Rémi, what are you talking about?"

"You have to come home. You're coming home, right?"

I felt like the worst granddaughter in the world, but I knew I wasn't going home. Not now.

I let the silence between us grow as I gave in to the thoughts racing through my head and felt them crash into me like a huge ocean wave: Ma, Pépère, making the National Team, and Tatiana rattling on about how great she was.

When I didn't answer, Rémi said, "You're upset, aren't you?"

"*Mais, oui* . . . it's just there's only four days left in camp, and these are like *crucial* days. . . ."

"Flora, what's wrong with you? Pépère's probably going to die. *Die*. Do you understand? Isn't Pépère more important than some stupid soccer camp?"

Stupid soccer camp?

Clearly Rémi still didn't get it. The big picture. The dream. Me. "Rémi," I told him. "I'm gonna have to think about this. *À plus tard!*" I didn't wait for his response. I pushed the hang-up button with my index finger and ripped off an e-mail to him.

> Did you really just lecture ME about DEATH???? And since when is trying out for a U.S. National Team 'some stupid soccer camp'? Piss off.

Pépère said to follow my dream. And that's what I planned to keep on doing. Screw Rémi.

I got up and started walking. I didn't know where I was going; I just needed to get away, needed to think. Pépère lay dying in a hospital bed, miles and miles away. It didn't feel real. What was I supposed to do? Stay at camp? Go home?

What if he died? Would I regret not going home?

Stop it, Flora! Stop it! He's not going to die. Not Pépère. He's too strong.

I touched the soccer ball charm. "Ma? I can't go home." The second the words tumbled out of my mouth, I knew in my heart that I couldn't. Part of me wanted to, but more of me knew that if I left ID Camp now, even after today's incredible play, I wouldn't make Matt's U-15 team.

Pépère would understand.

I came to Colorado to make the U.S. Under-15 Girls' National Soccer team, and that was what I was going to do. It wasn't much longer. In four days I'd be on Matt's team, and then I would go home.

I had to stay. I wanted to stay.

I just hoped Pa would let me.

Chapter 33
Psych Row

At dinner, I stood motionless in the hot food line while a group of boxers from South Africa swarmed around me. I'd lost both my appetite and my ability to move. And the boxers with their crooked noses and bulging biceps kind of freaked me out.

"You okay?" one of them asked me.

"You've got huge arms." *Flora!* I hid my face with my hands.

He laughed. "You're not too shabby on the muscle front either, girl." He put his tray down and extended his hand. "Hi. I'm Jengo, and I've got lots of muscles."

I shook his hand and laughed. "Hi. I'm Flora, and I've got to learn the difference between my inner voice and my outer voice."

We continued to chat as I filled my plate with salad, grilled chicken, and mashed potatoes. The smell of the food had brought back my appetite. Somewhere between the dessert table and the drinks I lost track of Jengo and his beefy friends, so I scanned the room for a friendly face. When I didn't see anyone I knew, I plunked myself down at an out-of-the-way booth.

I ate slowly. My head reeled. I was kind of relieved to be sitting alone. Poor Pépère. Lying in County General. At least Mémère was with him. And Pa.

"Mind if I join you?"

I couldn't place the woman standing in front of me. "Sure."

"I'm Charley. One of the sports psychologists here at the Academy."

"Oh, yeah," I said. "I've been meaning to come see you. My roommate has a hypnosis recording you made for her, Samantha Rhodes?"

"I can make a soccer one for you, if you'd like."

"That would be awesome."

"I heard about your grandfather." Who'd told Charley? Sally? That wrinkly lady at the desk who didn't know cell phones existed? "You want to swing by my office when you're done eating? We can talk about your options—"

"Options?" A million thoughts ran through my head. If I stayed, would my family forgive me? If I left, would Matt name me to the team? And, I hated to even think it, but what if Pépère died?

Charley rested her hand on my arm. "Yeah and, you know, how you're doing. It's a lot to take in, Flora."

I didn't want to go to Charley's office. I just wanted everything to go back to the way it was right after training, this afternoon. "Maybe in fifteen minutes?" I said.

Like I had a choice.

⚽   ⚽   ⚽

I took my time finishing dinner. When I was done I left the dining hall, walked along the main corridor, and thought about my conversation with Charley. What had she meant by *options*? Would she send me home? Could she? At the end of the long hallway, I turned the corner and almost fell flat on my face.

"Watch it," Tatiana said as I struggled to stay upright. She, Kaylee, and Zoe were camped out on the floor doing homework. I wanted to say, *Zoe, they think you're being a snot,* but I could have cared less about the Queen Bs's drama. I stepped over their books, legs, and water bottles. I walked farther down the hall, reading the nameplates on the doors as I went.

I could hear the Queen Bs behind me. "She's trolling psych row," Tatiana said. "Not a good sign . . . for her."

"Yeah, it looks like farm girl just can't handle the pressure," Kaylee said.

Zoe stayed silent. Whatever. I had bigger problems than the Queen Bs.

Chapter 34
Probably Best

Charley's office was at the very end of the long hallway. Several small lamps filled the room with warm, yellow light. I knocked on the open door, then entered the room.

Once I was inside, Charley gently closed the door behind me. "Take a seat," she said.

I considered the leather couch, but this being psych row, I didn't want Charley to get the wrong idea. I figured curling up in the overstuffed brown suede chair was a safer bet.

Charley reached for a cup of tea and took a sip. When the silence between us became too much, I blurted out, "I feel like the world's worst granddaughter, but I don't want to go home. Are you going to make me go home?"

"I'm not going to make you do anything, Flora. I just want you to know what your options are." Options. That word again. I reached down and played with a little nub of fabric on the armrest of my chair while Charley talked. "The Academy and these U-14 camps are pressure cookers. It's hard enough trying to survive camp. I want you to have a safe place to talk about your grandfather."

I nodded but didn't look up. "Thanks."

For the next hour we talked about Pépère. And Ma. And my feelings about soccer and how limited my opportunities were back home. It took awhile, but eventually I admitted to Charley—and myself—that I was terrified of making the wrong decision. I worried that if Pépère died, I'd never forgive myself for staying at camp. I wanted to be with my family, but something deep inside—Ma?—was telling me to stay.

"I think what's going on is you're becoming a grown-up," Charley said.

"I'm only fourteen," I said. "I'm a kid, not a grown-up."

"You are, and you aren't. You're a fourteen-year-old kid going after very grown-up goals."

I twisted the nub of fabric so hard it came off in my hand and left a tiny hole in the armrest. I moved my hand quickly to cover the hole. "The problem is, I'm not sure my family will understand. My cousin, he just assumed I'd leave. He called this a 'stupid soccer camp.'"

"How'd that make you feel?"

"Hurt." I picked my hand up just high enough to see if I really had torn a hole in Charley's chair. I had. "I'm mad, too . . . I mean, Pépère having a stroke and all, it just seems like something Pa should tell me, not Rémi."

Charley didn't say anything, so I kept on vomiting up my feelings.

"I spend so much time back home doing the right thing, being a good girl. For once, I want to do what's best for me. If I stay at camp, a lot of people in Acadia are going to be upset with me. They're not going to understand. But if I leave—" I wiped at a tear with my sleeve. "I'm not crying about Pépère.

I probably should be." I wiped my nose on my sleeve. "I'm cry-ing because I don't know what to do. I'm afraid of making the wrong decision."

"Grown-up goals and dreams come with grown-up re-sponsibilities and decisions." Charley got up from her seat, walked over to me, and squatted next to the big, cushy chair. "Ultimately, you have to make the decision, Flora. I can't tell you what to do."

"So it's my decision?"

She nodded.

"Okay. Can I call my dad?"

She nodded. "I'll wait outside. Take your time," she said. "And Flora, trust your gut."

A few minutes later, I was talking to Pa. I surprised myself by immediately blurting out that I wasn't coming home until the end of camp.

He said that was probably best. *Probably best?* What did that mean?

We talked for a total of maybe five minutes. There were lots of long silences on both ends of the phone. I wanted to tell Pa everything. How Tatiana called me a dump truck. How Matt picked on me. How I was the biggest girl at camp and everyone else played on travel teams. How I talked to Ma at night and how having the soccer ball charm helped. How I was afraid Pépère might die if I stayed at camp.

A big part of me couldn't wait to get off the phone, while another part hung on Pa's every word, hoping he'd tell me it was okay to stay—that I wouldn't regret it. I wanted to say, *Where's the Pa who sat on my bedroom floor and talked to me, really talked to me? Is he gone, again? Because I need him.*

When I sensed Pa was about to end our conversation, I barely whispered into the phone, "I'm sorry you have to go to County General."

"Me, too." He sighed. It was oddly comforting to know I wasn't the only one missing Ma tonight. "It's probably best you're not here right now." So that's what Pa had meant—it made me feel a little better knowing that.

But Pa sounded so sad. I wanted to tell him I loved him. The words just wouldn't come out, though. "Give Pépère my love," I said finally. "And tell Mémère I'm sorry and I'll get there as soon as I can."

"It's gonna be okay, Flora," Pa said. And then he was gone.

Chapter 35
Cocoa and Kisses

I found Charley in the main entry hall speaking with Sally. "There's my girl," Sally said. "How you holding up, sweetie?"

"Okay, thanks."

Charley put her hand on my shoulder. "You want to go back to my office?"

"No, I'm fine." I told them about the phone call, that I was staying, but I left out the part about Pa and me being reminded of Ma's death.

"I've got an idea," Sally said. "How about coming home with me for a couple hours? We can make popcorn and hang out. Get you away from here. What do you say?"

"Do I need permission?"

"You're looking at it," Charley said. "Go ahead. Just be back in time for lights out."

Sally lived a short drive from the Academy, but it felt worlds away from ID Camp. When we turned off the main road I had to crane my neck to see the tops of the tall pine trees that lined the long, dirt driveway. I spotted a deer deep in the woods. "Look." I pointed to my right.

Sally stopped the car. I rolled down my window, and she leaned across me and said, "Evening, Bambi. How goes it?"

The deer stopped eating a leaf, tilted her head to look at us, and then scampered deeper into the woods. "It's feeding time," Sally said. "Sometimes at this hour we'll see half a dozen of them."

"She's beautiful."

"Fattening up just in time for hunting season," Sally said.

"No!" I looked at Sally. "Tell me you don't shoot deer."

"Okay then, I don't shoot deer."

"Good."

"But I know people who do."

"You're terrible," I said. We were still laughing when Sally pulled up in front of her house. She told me she and her husband had built it themselves. The house was tucked into a clearing of pine trees. It looked like a life-size version of one of those Lincoln Log houses Rémi and I used to build on the living-room floor.

Sally flung open the front door of the house and called out, "Cocoa! Kisses!" She turned to me and smiled. "I hope you like dogs."

Before I could answer, two Labrador retrievers, one black, one brown, barreled into the mudroom and jumped on us. I got down on my knees to accept their sloppy, wet kisses. "They're so cute. Can we take them for a w-a-l-k?"

"Clever girl spelling out the magic word," she said. "All right, but just so you know, they're going to w-a-l-k us."

"Fine by me," I said and stepped aside as the dogs clamored over one another to get out the front door. They ran into the clearing, rolled in the grass, and barked at us. "I think they want us to get with the program," I said. "We're too pokey."

Cocoa and Kisses led us toward an opening in the trees. "My husband cut this trail so we could ride our mountain bikes through the woods. He's out there somewhere right now with his buddies."

Kisses picked up a stick and tried to put it in my hand. "Pushy little one, aren't you?" I scratched her ears. She plopped down on her side so I'd rub her belly.

Sally pushed her toe under Kisses's backside. "Up you go, lazybones."

I threw the stick as far as I could down the trail, and the dogs took off after it. We spent the next hour ambling along the mountain bike paths. I wasn't sure who was having more fun, the dogs or me. At one point, a group of mountain bikers rode up behind us. They joked with Sally as they slowly passed us on the narrow track. One of them said, "Did you hear what happened to Simon?"

"Tell me he didn't break any bones," Sally said.

"No, but he's got a whopper of a story to tell you."

"As long as he's not hurt," Sally said. And we laughed and waved as the bikers took off down the path ahead of us.

"That looks like fun," I said.

"Oh yeah, it's fun . . . until you crash." I crinkled up my face. "See this scar?" Sally pointed to a perfectly round white dot the size of a dime on her calf. "That was from a twig. And this one on my back . . ." She hoisted her shirttail. "A tree stump."

"Ouch," I said. "Seriously, I'm sticking to soccer."

When we got back to the house, Simon, Sally's husband, was in the kitchen. He'd made a big bowl of popcorn. Simon was from Australia and I noticed, just like with Matt, I had to listen hard to understand his accent. The three of us sat on stools around the kitchen island while Simon told us about his mountain bike ride. "So, I'm cruising around this corner, and what do you know, there's a bear on the trail."

Sally and I covered our eyes.

"The little nong just stood there," Simon said. "I jammed on my brakes. Just about binned it."

Sally turned to me. "I'll translate. A nong's a fool; binned means crashed."

"Thanks," I said and reached for another fistful of popcorn. "So what happened? Did the bear run away?"

"I wish," Simon said. "Nah, he waddled right up to me and sniffed my shoe."

"Oh, please," Sally said. "Your stinky feet? Did he die on the spot?"

"I rolled away before he could get a good whiff . . . or a good nibble."

Sally rolled her eyes at her husband.

"It was freaky," he said. "He was a wee cub, so I figured I better haul out of there before mama bear showed up." Simon threw a piece of popcorn in the air and caught it in his mouth. "And here I am, good as gold."

Before long it was time for Sally to drive me back to the Academy. Simon walked us to the car. He leaned down and gave me a big hug. "You're good value, Flor-o," he said. "Come back anytime."

It felt so good to be wrapped up in his strong arms. I wanted to tell Sally and Simon all about my phone call with Pa, but I just climbed into the passenger seat of Sally's car. "I'll come back, but I'm not getting on a mountain bike."

"Fair enough," he said. "Cheers, mate."

Sally tooted the horn and we pulled away. I looked back through the side view mirror. Simon stood on the front porch, one hand resting on Cocoa's head, the other waving good-bye. Simon and Sally hadn't asked me about Pépère, camp, or soccer, but I felt like they knew what was going through my head. I felt understood. I felt great.

When I returned to Beijing, Samantha was asleep. I didn't want to wake her, so I undressed and brushed my teeth in the dark. When I went to pull the covers back, I felt Samantha's teddy bear propped up against my pillow. A note lay across his chest. I had to hold it near the window to read it.

Dear Flora,
Thought you might need Teddy tonight.
Lots of love,
Samantha

This place was feeling more and more like home.

Chapter 36
Guilt by Association

The next morning we faced off against Tatiana, Kaylee, and their Team B teammates. Tatiana and I were in our usual positions on the front line at target forward. Kaylee was one of her wings, while—irony of all ironies—Zoe was one of mine.

From the opening whistle, Tatiana and Kaylee started in with their psycho comments. I tried to ignore them. I figured even if they knew the real reason I was in Charley's office they'd still pick on me. That's just the kind of girls they were. As best I could tell, only Charley, Sally, and Samantha knew about Pépère. All I wanted to do was play soccer and forget about everything else.

During a restart, while everyone gathered near Team B's goal to set up for a corner kick, Sperry told the two of them to leave me alone. "What's your problem?" Tatiana said. "We're not talking to you."

"My problem is you're being mean. Flora's never been anything but nice to you guys." A vein in Sperry's forehead throbbed with every word out of her mouth. "We're supposed to work together, not against each other. Just cut it out."

Sperry took a step back toward me, instinctively raised her right hand, and we high-fived each other. "Thanks," I said.

"You'd do it for me," she said.

I hadn't thought about it before, but, yes, I would do the same for Sperry. We were friends and teammates, and that's what friends and teammates do.

Thanks to Sperry, Tatiana and Kaylee backed off. If only Matt had, too. He pointed out everything I did wrong, which seemed to be . . . everything. "Crack on, Flora," he said, or "Any danger?" as in, any danger of you moving today. And if he thought I was spacing out he yelled, "Switch on!"

When Matt, for what felt like the hundredth time, said, "Any danger?" about my being slow to the action, Tatiana pounced. "Talk about danger. She's like an elephant coming down the field."

I'd had enough. Enough of the Queen Bs. Enough of Matt. Enough of feeling I should be home with Pépère. And enough of Pa's sadness. A high ball came toward me; I went up against Kaylee for the header. Kaylee went for the ball; I went for Kaylee. She got to the ball first, but as we came back down to the ground I threw an elbow that caught her square in the left breast. Kaylee crumpled to the ground, her hands cupping her chest. I stood over her and said, "That was for the elephant comment."

"But I didn't say it. Tatiana did."

"Guilt by association," I said and jogged back toward the action. I caught my *teammate* Zoe's eye. She giggled nervously.

The coaches had seen my cheap shot, but I didn't care. I braced myself for a whistle, or a reprimand, but none came.

I raced up the right flank. Sperry passed me the ball. I

bobbled it, before sending it square to Zoe. I heard Matt say, "One touch, Flora, not one hundred." I was so angry I could have strangled him.

That afternoon when we played Team C, Matt ignored me. At first I wasn't sure which was worse, being yelled at or being ignored, but pretty quickly I decided I wanted him to yell at me. If he yelled, it meant he was aware of me—and if he was aware of me, it meant I was still in the mix to make the U-15s. Running up and down the pitch in my silent vacuum, I started to wonder if my elbow to the breast had been worth it.

I spent a good portion of the second half on the bench, watching my teammates keep the ball in Team C's final third. It gave me time to think. To plan. The longer camp went on, the more I knew I *had* to make the U-15s. If I didn't make the team, get out of Maine, my soccer future was in serious jeopardy. The next few years were crucial; if I wanted to keep up with the Sperrys and Nikeshas of the world, I had to play year-round. But how could I do that with no club soccer or ODP in northern Maine? I was still five years away from playing college soccer—so until then, I had to make the U-15s so I could keep improving. That meant no more playing basketball for Acadia Central in the winter. I had to run and lift weights and find a way to do soccer drills in the barn when there was snow on the ground.

I also had to deal with my body. The reality was, I was tall and big boned. And despite what the Queen Bs said, I wasn't fat. I was a big, strong Dupre girl. It was time to change how I used my body on the field. I thought back to my elbow smashing into Kaylee's breast and flinched. Okay, not my finest moment.

"Flora," Matt said. "Jog on."

I joined my teammates on the forward line. *All right girl,* I told myself, *it's time to love the largeness.*

Zoe dished off to me and I cleared it with a beautiful long ball up the length of the pitch. I'll put on more muscle, I vowed, and get in better shape. And I'll get that soccer hypnosis recording from Charley.

With only three and a half days left of camp, I knew I had to stay focused, had to stay on Matt's good side.

Pépère was depending on me to give it my best shot. He deserved that.

Chapter 37
Sisters

That evening Sperry, Nikesha, and I took over the leather chairs in one of the lounge areas just off the dining hall. Once we'd settled in, I told my friends about Pépère's stroke and that I wasn't going home.

"Do you think I'm selfish, you know, a bad person for staying here?" I asked them.

Sperry sat up tall, and the leather squeaked under her butt. All three of us howled with laughter. "That was *not* a fart," she said. "See." She scooted her butt back and forth trying to make the sound again. "I can't do it." She looked at us with red cheeks. "Honestly, that wasn't a fart."

"Are you sure about that?" said a guy's voice behind us.

We all spun around. *Logan!* How long had he been standing there?

Logan spread his arms and bowed at the waist. "Ladies."

Samantha jumped out from behind him. "*Hola* chickies." She climbed onto the arm of Nikesha's chair. "Girls' night out?"

"Yeah," I said. "What's up?"

Logan reached over the back of my chair to rub my shoulders. "Not much," he said. "Just wanted to come by, see how you're doing."

"I'm good." I felt the weight of his hands on my shoulders, wished he wouldn't stop, until I saw Nikesha and Sperry exchange a glance.

"I heard about your grandfather," he said. "I'm sorry."

"Thanks," I replied as I shot Samantha a disappointed look. She shrugged her shoulders and smiled, not getting it. I knew Samantha was a talker, that she liked to know everything about everyone at the ISA, but I never expected her to use my secrets as currency in the ISA gossip mill.

It was too late now. But I knew one thing, I'd never spill *her* secrets.

Samantha pretended to smother me with hugs. "Love you too, Roomie," she said.

I'm gonna kill you later, I thought to myself.

Logan knelt down by my chair. "I just wanted to make sure you're okay. We're a long way from home, so us New Englanders, we have to watch out for each other."

"Thanks." I wanted to say more. But what? I wasn't used to guys like this. Or *any* guys for that matter. So I just smiled. When he reached out and held my hand, a voice inside my head said, *Don't let go.*

But Samantha broke the spell when she jumped on Logan's back. "What do you say we leave these girls alone and find some trouble to get into?"

"Your wish is my command," Logan said and then turned to the three of us. "Ladies. Enjoy your farting."

When they were out of earshot, Sperry said, "Oh. My. Goodness. He's gorgeous."

"Yeah," I said. "He's sweet."

"Sweet?" Nikesha said. "Sister, he's delicious."

"Samantha seems kind of into him—" Sperry began.

"Oh, no, not like that," I said. "They've known each other since they were little kids. He used to be a gymnast. She calls him her long-lost brother."

"Really?" Sperry said, sounding unconvinced.

"Yeah, she's been through a lot—injuries, pressure from her parents—and Logan's been there for her. And seriously, the only thing Samantha's into right now is making the Pacific Rim Championships team." It was time to change the subject. "And speaking of teams, we've only got three days to make the U-15s."

"Okay," Sperry said. "Enough about boys." She turned and faced me. "Flora, I'm really sorry about your grandfather, but you made the right decision to stay at camp. Going home won't change his situation."

"But what if they don't understand?" I said.

"Who's they?" Nikesha asked.

"Everyone in Acadia."

"You mean like the whole town?" I nodded. "Girl, you're lucky people care about you. I come from Brooklyn. I'm gone, no one notices," Nikesha said.

"That's sad," I said.

"Is what it is."

"Living in a small town, everyone knows your business. And everyone has an opinion. No one in Acadia, except maybe my coach, gets me. They think I'm weird because all I want to do is play soccer." I fiddled with my ponytail. I still hadn't heard from Rémi since my last e-mail. *Had I really told him to piss off?* "I know what they say behind my back, 'All she wants to do is play sports. That poor thing, with no mother to teach her how to be feminine—'"

"That's ridiculous. You're incredibly feminine," Sperry said.

"Wow." I was speechless. No one had ever called me feminine before. "Thanks."

Nikesha stretched out in her chair so her legs hung over one arm and her back over the other. "Boyfriends," she said, hanging her head back and trying to touch her long braids to the floor, "are drama. No time for that."

I thought of Logan's hands resting on my shoulders, how I could feel his warmth through my shirt. I tried to shake the memory from my head. "Yeah," I added, "even if they do look like Abercrombie & Fitch models." I didn't want to like Logan. I couldn't afford to like him. Not with just three days left to make Matt's U-15 Girls' National Team.

"Give me a soccer ball over a boyfriend any day," Sperry said.

"You guys are amazing," I said.

"We get each other," Sperry said, like it was the most obvious thing in the world.

"My sistuhs," Nikesha said in an exaggerated New York accent and high-fived us.

I'd never had anyone call me their sister. I felt like I was glowing from the inside out. "You're right, Sper'," I said. "I have to stay. This camp's the most important thing that's ever happened to me. It's my chance."

"It's *our* chance," Nikesha added.

Sitting with Nikesha and Sperry, I sensed my confidence coming back. I felt especially good when the conversation turned to the importance of body size and strength.

"I don't get you white girls and your obsession with being skinny," Nikesha said. She turned to tall, slender, perfect Sperry. "No offense."

"None taken . . . yet."

"For real, where I come from, curves are what it's about. Skinny, little boy-bodies just aren't considered sexy." She stood up and showed us her backside. "I've got a big, muscular butt." She slapped it for emphasis. Then she puffed out her chest. "I come from a long line of big-chested women. That's just who I am. I look at Mama, my cousins, I see my future. It's big, it's bold, and it's beautiful." We laughed as Nikesha sat back down and intentionally squeaked her butt against the leather seat.

"I wish I could feel that good about my body," I said. "I come from big women, too. We're farm girls, two hundred years' worth. But it's been hard here—being so much bigger than everyone else."

"Don't worry," Sperry said. "By the time we all come back for U-15 training camp you won't be the only tall girl. I promise."

"Which part do you promise?" Nikesha asked. "That we'll all come back—"

"Yes!" Sperry and I shouted.

Then the three of us said it together. "We'll all come back."

We gathered up our bags and prepared to say good night. "One day," Sperry said, "we're going to be telling a reporter from *Sports Illustrated* about the night we sat around at the International Sports Academy and realized we were sisters."

"Sistuhs," Nikesha corrected.

"Right, sistuhs," Sperry said. "We're gonna be the next generation of Mia Hamms, Julie Foudys, and Brandi Chastains."

"I want to be Brandi," Nikesha said, "so I can take off my shirt."

"All yours," I said, thinking back to my three-year-old mortified self.

"Group hug." We dropped our bags and embraced.

Ma should have been there. She would have loved it.

Chapter 38
Engage Brain More

The next morning I woke up to an e-mail from Pa. Pa, who never wrote e-mails.

> Pépère had a pretty good night. Eyes still closed and not
> talking yet, but he seems to know when we're in the room.
> He smiles sometimes when Mémère holds his hand. Three
> days to go for you, right? Give us an update later today
> and we'll read it to Pépère.

I read the e-mail on my way out to the field. I couldn't believe Pa knew there were just three days left in camp. It was good to get an update on Pépère, but as I laced up my boots I knew I had to put him—and everyone in Acadia—out of my mind for the next few hours.

Once we started playing, Matt went all silent on us. From the field, he looked like a clipboard-gripping statue someone had placed on the touchline. His eyes were the only things that moved. Back and forth, back and forth. Every once in a while he'd jot down a note or lean in for a secret conversation with another coach, but mostly he just stared straight ahead.

Matt's silence drove me crazy. With just today, tomorrow, and Sunday left in ID Camp, I needed to know if I was still on his U-15 radar. So I walked up to him during a water break and tried to make small talk. "Hi, Matt." I grabbed a paper cup and filled it with water. "How's it going?"

He looked me up and down. "I've been watching you, lass, and the reality is you're big and you're slow."

I wanted to scream, but I didn't. I reminded myself that Matt was the only thing standing between me and my dream of playing for the U.S.A.

"Flora, it's up to you to figure out how to make your size work for you."

Say something! that little voice in my head screamed. But I didn't know what to say, so I just mumbled, "O-okay."

I watched Matt walk away. When he got to the end of the bench, he turned back around. "I'm not convinced you want this."

"I do," I said a little too desperately. *If I didn't want this I'd be on my way home,* I thought. *To be with my grandfather. Who's probably gonna die! DIE!*

I crumpled my paper cup and threw it in the trash bucket. I looked up and caught Rainey's eye. She gave me a thumbs-up. At least one of the coaches believed in me. But Rainey was the U-14 Girls' National Team ID Camp coach; Matt was the one I had to win over.

I went back out to the front line with a single purpose in mind—to convince Matt how much I wanted to be on the U-15s. When we had the ball I hustled forward to help set up the other forwards to score, and when the ball was in our end I raced back to support the defenders. My touches were clean, my passes crisp. But I was tired from the sheer volume of drills and games, and it started to show more and more as the half progressed. Twice Kaylee won possession by faking me out with body movements that earlier in the week I wouldn't have fallen for. I was frustrated, but mostly I was exhausted. All that up and back, superwoman, team player stuff had sapped me. I needed a rest.

When the referee blew the whistle to end the first half, I made a beeline for the bench. I had to get off my legs. But on my way there, Matt waved me over to where he stood on the sideline. "Why'd you let Kaylee push you around out there?"

I focused my hands and eyes on un-tucking and re-tucking my jersey. "I was tired."

"You've got to be more clever," he said. "It's not just about muscling your way around people. Especially when you're tired."

"Matt, I'm trying my best. I've never been up against a whole team of good players," I said. "Sometimes I forget I'm not playing in a high school game."

"You're going to need to play more this year if you want to remain in the national team player pool."

"I know," I said. "You've got to believe me, I want this more than anything. I do. Right now, I'm just trying to play the best I can at camp. I'll worry about the other stuff when I get home."

Matt pulled a pen from his pocket and wrote, *Engage Brain More* on his clipboard. He showed it to me, underlined it, and then walked away.

I felt tears flood my eyes. Of all our conversations, this had been one of the most civil. He'd been a little mean, but he'd also been a little nice. Before I knew what was happening, I felt Rainey's arm around my shoulders. She gently led me away from the other girls and coaches. By the time we reached the backside of an equipment shed, I was crying so hard my chest heaved and I gasped for breath.

"It's okay." Rainey hugged me. "Let it out."

"I'm s-s-s-sorry." Rainey smoothed her hand over my hair and continued to hold me. "What's wrong with me?" My words came out in hiccups. "That's the nicest he's been in a while, and what do I do? Bawl my eyes out."

"I think he scares you." I nodded into Rainey's neck. She laughed and said, "Hey, he scares me, too."

"Yeah, but does he make you feel like a big, fat loser?"

"All day. Every day," she said.

"For real?" I lifted my head off her shoulder to look at her. "Are you just saying that to make me feel better?"

"Flora, Matt coached in the English Premier League. He coached Beckham and Paul Scholes. Look at me; I'm a club coach from Boston. I've never even been to Old Trafford Stadium . . . the Theatre of Dreams . . . that place was Matt's office for seven years."

"Yeah, but you're such a good coach." Rainey gave me a quick, hard hug. I leaned against the equipment shed. My tears had stopped, but every once in a while my chest fluttered and my breath came in feathery spurts. "He hates me," I said.

Rainey sat on the ground and leaned against the shed. She motioned for me to slide down and join her. "Matt's not here to be your friend. He's here to find the girls with the most potential." She nudged my boot with her own. "Did you ever think all his tough-guy stuff might be a way to test you? To see how strong you are? To see how much you really want to play for the U.S.A.?"

"You think he's testing me?"

"It's one way to look at it." Rainey glanced around to see if anyone was within earshot of us. "Between you and me, Matt thinks you're incredible. Says you're the only one out there with a soccer brain."

I'd never heard that term before. "What's that?"

"It means you live in the moment. You see what's happening on the pitch and you react quickly. You adapt."

"Isn't everyone like that?"

Rainey threw her head back and laughed. "Hardly. Half the time, there's a bunch of jerseys running around out there and nobody in them. True soccer brains are rare." She put her hands on my head and pretended to massage my brain. "And Matt's always saying you've got one heck of a left peg."

"A left peg?"

"Leg. A good left shot," Rainey said. "He loves how you use your body to defend the ball. I know it feels like he's hard on you, but sometimes coaches are hardest on the players they expect the most from. Matt says you remind him of his daughter."

"What—" I flashed back to the photo pinned to Matt's office wall.

"Yeah, high praise, right?" Rainey stood up, extended her hand to me. "Like I said, maybe he's testing you." She pulled me up to my feet.

"I never did like tests," I said. "But I always pass them."

"I like your attitude, Flora."

⚽ ⚽ ⚽

That night I got an e-mail from Uncle Al, Rémi's dad. I was afraid to read it. I still hadn't heard from Rémi since I'd told him to piss off.

The old guy's gonna live. Woke up tonight. Asked about you. Told him you were kickin' butt. You are, right? Love ya!!

Uncle Al always knew how to make me laugh. *Yeah*, I thought, *I'm kickin' butt*.

Chapter 39
Nightmare

The next morning, I woke up to an e-mail from Pa's brother Uncle Henri.

> Here's a lame-o poem I wrote in honor of your next-to-last
> day of camp . . .
> Roses are Red.
> Violets are Blue.
> Get out of Bed.
> Camp ends in Two.
> Days, that is. Told you it was lame! Everyone's pulling for
> you, Flora. Go get 'em! Make us proud!! Can't wait to hear
> all about ISA when you get home.
> Love, Uncle H

During warm-ups, I struggled to get my muscles going—
the light rain and cool weather didn't help. No matter how
much I jogged and stretched, I couldn't get the previous day's
games out of my legs. I was stiff, I was sore, and I was tired.

Shortly after we broke off to do flying changes, a series of 1 v. 1 contests with small goals, my right hamstring seized up. It happened so fast it felt like a dream. Well, more like a nightmare.

Tony, the head physical therapist, ran onto the pitch and quickly relieved the muscle cramp with some massage. The pain was so intense that all I could focus on was how wet and muddy my uni was getting from the field. I must have been in shock because I didn't once try to stand up and get back to training. I lay flat on my stomach and silently watched the circle of coaches and assistants around me grow larger. All those adults crowding around, looking down on me, made me claustrophobic, even though I could only see their feet. When I focused on what they were saying, I got truly frightened.

"That's it. She's done for the day."

"We should have kept the girls inside this morning. It's too cold."

"Let's get her out of here."

Tony helped me stand up. I tried to walk, but my hamstring cramped again. Tony mashed his fingers around in the muscles and it released. I wiped tears from my eyes with my jersey sleeve as I watched my teammates continue the 1 v. 1 drill.

Then I came to my senses and panicked. "I can play." I looked up at Tony and pleaded, "I've only got today and to-morrow to prove myself!"

"You're spending the day in the training room, kiddo, whether you want to or not. Coaches' orders."

"Which coach?" I asked. "I'll talk to him." I looked toward the coaches. "Or her."

"All of them," Tony said. "For the first time, they're in agreement about something." He helped me into a golf cart. It was painted red, white, and blue, like the ISA buses. As we slowly chugged up the hill toward the Academy buildings I couldn't help but wonder if the Women's National Team had their own golf carts.

I'd never been in the Academy trainers' room, even though I'd walked by it every day I'd been at camp. Back home I never got injured. Tony threw open the door and helped me walk to one of the massage tables. I crinkled up my nose. The room smelled like a combination of menthol, sweat, and chlorine. "This place smells." I pinched my nose with my fingers.

"You bet it smells," Tony said. "Like hard work."

"No, like dirty socks floating in a swimming pool."

Tony laughed as he scooted me back on the table. "You'll see," he said, "the hardest work at the ISA goes on within these four walls."

Tony picked me up and placed me facedown on the leather massage table. "Jeez, what are you, a WWE wrestler?" I said. "Tony the Titan. He lifts mighty farm girls with one arm."

"Something like that," he said and put an ice pack on my hamstring. After twenty minutes, he took it off and warmed my skin back up and then gently worked the kink out of my muscle. "It's not a major injury," Tony said. "But we need to see this as a warning." He squatted down next to me so we could talk eye to eye. "We need to figure out why this muscle failed and prevent it from happening in the future. You can't afford to have muscle pulls, even minor ones, at this level."

Tony alternated cold and massage a couple more times while we talked about strength training, off-field conditioning, agility exercises, and nutrition. The more he talked, the harder I listened. "This is embarrassing," I said. "But until I came to the Academy, I didn't know there was more to soccer than playing and stretching."

"Don't be embarrassed. Why would you know? ID Camp is all about education, about learning what it takes to become an elite athlete." Tony wrapped an ice pack in towels and placed it on my leg. "You can't just play soccer. You've got to work hard off the pitch, too. You're in the early stages of your career and you're young, so this is the perfect time to add these elements. This is what will help you make the jump to a national team."

I held the ice pack down with my hand and rolled over enough so that I could see Tony when I spoke to him. "So even though Matt's going to announce the next cut at any moment, you're saying I should see my injury as a good thing?"

"Believe it or not, that's exactly what I'm saying."

I laughed with Tony, but inside I was terrified. "Okay, but what if Matt cuts me because of my hamstring?"

"He sees the big picture, trust me."

Trust me? Tony seemed like a good guy, but I wasn't ready to trust him with my future. Tomorrow was the last day of camp, and I had to make the U-15s. I was excited to learn about off-field conditioning, I just wished it were under different circumstances.

When Tony finished massaging my leg, he wiped the massage oil off with a warm towel and pulled me up to a seated position. "Spending time in the trainers' room, it's all part of being an elite athlete. We like to think you kids couldn't make it without us."

He led me to the far end of the room, where a squishy

blue mat covered the floor. I wondered what the other girls were doing. Had the coaches forgotten about me? Tony and I took off our socks and shoes, and he put me through a series of stretching exercises. "You're tight in your hamstrings," he said. "You've also got lots of little muscle imbalances. Like most girls, you've got overdeveloped quadriceps and under-developed hamstrings."

"Can I fix this?"

"Sure, it's actually quite easy," he said. "The most important thing is to strengthen your hamstrings. This will help prevent knee injuries—which, of course, are the most common injuries for girls in your sport."

For the next hour, Tony worked with me on a series of boxes, balls, and balance boards. He taught me some exercises to stretch my hamstrings and hip flexors and others to strengthen my core muscles. After we went over ways to develop my hamstrings, we took a break, and I lay facedown again on the massage table. I closed my eyes.

And that's the last I remembered.

A half hour later, I rolled over and realized the ice was gone and I was snuggled up under a fleece blanket. I looked at Tony through bleary eyes. "Where am I?"

"Inside a sock, floating in a pool," he answered.

"Need food," I said. "Now."

"Only if you let me join you."

Chapter 40
Validation

On the way to the dining hall I checked my e-mail. Mémère!

MA CHERIE! PÉPÈRE'S NOT OUT OF THE WOODS YET, BUT HE'S DOING MUCH BETTER. HE WANTS YOU TO KNOW HE'S PROUD OF YOU. WE ALL ARE!

In the dining hall, Tony and I sat with Charley, the sports psychologist. "I heard you had a pretty rotten morning," she said.

"Yes and no," I said and shoved a roll into my mouth. "I mean, it stinks to tweak my hamstring and miss training, but I learned so much about off-field conditioning from Tony." *And Pépère's not mad at me for staying at ID Camp.*

"That reminds me," Charley said. "I've got something for you." She reached into her bag, pulled out a nutrition bar. "Not that." A cell phone. "Not that. Where is it?" She rummaged around some more before coming up with a memory stick.

"Is that the hypnosis recording?"

Charley nodded yes.

"Thanks," I said.

"I've heard about these recordings," Tony said. "How do they work?"

"They work off the premise that to be a champion you have to think like a champion," Charley explained. "They put you in a trance, or deeply relaxed state, and help you focus, relax, and get in the zone. And when you're there, you unconsciously hear subliminal messages embedded in the tracks."

"That sounds like mind control," I said, only half-joking.

"It's not. What I do is encourage you to believe in yourself, to know you are strong, confident, and can do anything you want. The reality is your body will only take you so far. Your mind has to do the rest. These recordings help train your brain."

"That's so interesting," Tony said. "Especially for a guy like me who comes from the physical side of sport."

"As an athlete you focus so much on physical training that it's easy to forget the power of thought," Charley said. "At the Elite level—at any level really—training your mind can be just as important as training your body. Bottom line, you'll never become stronger than your mind believes is possible."

"But it's not like hypnosis recordings take the place of physical training, right?" Tony said.

"No, not at all. You still have to put in the hard work; it's just that when you listen to the recording on a regular basis it helps you break through mental blocks and achieve things you never imagined possible."

"This is amazing," I said. "You guys are amazing." I couldn't believe how lucky I was to be at ID Camp. Before arriving at the ISA I never imagined so much went into being an elite soccer player. I looked around the bustling dining hall and said, "I hope the kids who get to live and train year-round at ISA know how fortunate they are."

"I think some of them do," Charley said. "But the life of an elite athlete, it's not for everyone."

"I used to dream about wearing a U.S.A. jersey. A real one. For a real national team," I said. "I used to think it would be the best thing in the whole world."

"And now that you have the training jersey—" Tony said.

"Oh man, it's great, don't get me wrong, but now I want more. I want to wear a game jersey—I want to live the life. I want to eat, sleep, and dream soccer."

"You can start by listening to your hypnosis recording to-day," Charley suggested.

"Done!" I said, anxious to get back to my room.

"Flora, you've got the right attitude to make it as an elite soccer player. Do you realize that?" Tony asked.

I couldn't believe what I was hearing. "Ayuh," I said, suddenly embarrassed that someone at the freakin' International Sports Academy had just validated my dream, my goal.

Tony slapped me on the back. "After rest period I want you to jump in the ice bath and do some light stretching. You do that, you can play tomorrow."

Play, I will.

Chapter 41
Hard Cheese

The next morning I woke up and couldn't believe it was the last day of U-14 camp. The past two weeks had flown by. When I turned my phone on, it went crazy downloading new e-mails from home.

You know what to do, Flora. Be strong. U-15s here you come! Coach Roy

Good luck today. Hope your leg's feeling better. Let us know how it goes. Pa

PEELING THE APPLES FOR YOUR PIE NOW. WE'LL SHARE IT WITH PÉPÈRE IN THE HOSPITAL TOMORROW NIGHT WHEN YOU GET HOME. LOVE YA!

There was nothing from Rémi—which was hardly surprising after what I'd said to him—but Rémi and I had never gone this long without making up after a fight. As Mémère would say, it was time for one of us—me!—to bridge the gap, so I opened a new e-mail and started to type.

> Cuz, I'm a jerk. Once again I let my obsession with soccer come between us. ☹ I'm sorry I took it out on you. Forgive me?

At breakfast I was thinking about my hamstring and not paying attention to where I was going in the food line, when I ran right smack into Matt. I nearly dumped my loaded tray down his shirt. If it had been anyone else, I probably would have laughed. But this was Matt. "S-s-sorry," I said.

"Mind yourself, kidda," he said and looked down at my tray. "Good to see you passed on the Lucky Charms and went for the porridge."

At least that's what I thought he said. That darn English accent, I still couldn't understand half of what he said. In Matt's mouth, porridge, which I guessed meant oatmeal, came out sounding like POOR-reed-juh.

"I'm not a big sugar-cereal girl," I said and then looked at him and smiled. "Hey, I got the all-clear from Tony. I can play today."

Matt reached for a banana. "Right, we need to talk about that."

My stomach dropped. Matt didn't say anything else, as he sliced the banana into his bowl. I wasn't sure if our conversation was over. Had I been dismissed? Should I stay? Should I go? I didn't know what to do, so I kept walking down the breakfast line with him. I watched him pour milk on his cereal, butter a bagel, and take a sip of orange juice. I felt like a complete idiot standing around waiting for Matt to speak.

Or not. Finally he turned to me and said, "Drop by my office at eight thirty."

"Okay, great, sure." I gave him my best Sperry I-am-so-confident smile, turned, and walked away. When I reached Nikesha and Sperry I dropped my tray on the table and plopped myself into a chair.

"Nice move crashing into Matt. What'd he say?" Sperry asked.

"He's cutting me. I know it. I'll have to go to the far fields with the castoffs."

Nikesha shook her index finger in front of her face. "Take it back. Take it back."

"What?" I said. "He is. And all because of one stupid hamstring cramp." I lifted a spoonful of mushy oatmeal toward my mouth. "I have to go to his office at eight thirty." I jammed the spoon into my mouth. "He's gonna cut me. I know it."

Nikesha smacked her hand on the red Formica table. My spoon clattered to the floor, Sperry's orange juice splattered, and some of the kids at nearby tables turned to see what was going on. Nikesha waved her finger again, but this time she did it in front of *my* face. "No, you didn't just say that."

The look on her face and the tone of her voice surprised me. "Why are you mad at me?" I said.

"Because you're being ridiculous." Nikesha stared at me and then shook her head. "You think Matt's gonna throw you off the team? Get real."

Sperry sat up straight and rested her fork on the edge of her plate. "It's true. Flora, you're one of the best players at camp. Nikesha's right; you're overreacting." She dabbed at her lips with a napkin. "Maybe he's going to give you good news. Did you consider that?"

"I don't want to talk about it," I said. "Let's just eat."

My friends knew better than to push the point. Sperry changed the subject and told us about her little sister. Apparently Melissa, or Li'l Missy, as Sperry called her, was driving their parents crazy back home. She insisted on sleeping in Sperry's bed and wearing Sperry's favorite Mia Hamm jersey. She even tried to get on Sperry's school bus when it stopped in front of their house.

"Wait," I said, "does she even go to school yet?"

"No. She starts pre-K next year. I guess the bus stopped at the end of the driveway, and the next thing my mom knew, the driver was honking his horn like crazy. Mom looked out the window and there was Li'l Missy, standing on the steps of the bus. She was even carrying my backpack."

"What did your mom do?" Nikesha asked.

"Went out there and physically pulled her off the bus. I think the poor kid's still screaming."

Nikesha laughed. "Li'l Missy can come by my house any day she wants to go to school for me. I won't fight her. I'll push her right out the door."

"You're terrible," I said.

"Careful. My mom might take you up on that," Sperry said.

"Does Li'l Missy come to your games?" Nikesha asked.

"Yeah, she's our good luck mascot. She loves to wear our uni and run up and down the touchlines. The shorts hang down to the tops of her shoes and the short sleeves cover her little hands."

"That's so cute," I said. "It must be cool to have a little sister."

"Yeah, except when I have to babysit. My parents love that I'm old enough to stay home alone with her."

"Oh, yeah," said Nikesha, "because you've got so many parties to go to. What a bummer."

"Ha-ha," Sperry said.

"Admit it, you're home every night," Nikesha said, "watching Fox Soccer Channel—"

Sperry threw her arms in the air and said, "Busted," and we all laughed.

I knew what my friends were doing, and I appreciated it. I was terrified to talk to Matt after breakfast, but I felt better knowing Nikesha and Sperry believed in my talent. Maybe, just maybe, they were right and Matt had good news for me.

I was late, so I jogged over to Matt's office. I passed Logan and a few guys on their way to the weight room. I smiled, called "Hi," and low-fived Logan as I ran by. I didn't have time for boys today. When I passed my crying bench I winced at the memory of telling Matt that Ma was dead.

I took a deep breath, stood up tall and confident, and walked through Matt's open office door.

"Hullo, Goldilocks," he said, and I gave him a puzzled look. "I thought you American kids loved that story." Matt got up from behind his desk. "You know you ate POOR-reed-juh for breakfast and now you're here to see the Big Bad Wolf."

"You're not big." I crossed my fingers behind my back and hoped Matt realized that was a joke.

He laughed. "Good show. As Rainey would say, Flora, 1; Matt, 0."

We sat down, me on a big leather chair near the door, Matt on a metal folding chair in front of his desk. "After your injury yesterday," he said, "we decided to make some changes."

Please don't cut me. Please don't cut me. Please—

"We're switching you from right striker to left back."

I felt like I'd been smacked in the forehead with a rubber mallet. *He was moving me from forward to defender? From the right side of the field to the left? Was he crazy?*

Matt stared at me. "What do you think?"

"I . . . I . . . I don't understand. I'm right-footed," I said. "I've always been a striker."

"You've got a crackin' left peg, Flora. And your size and strength make more sense on defense."

How could he move me from the prime scoring position to defense? *Defense?*

And then it hit me. I was still in the mix to make the U-15s. I should have been happy. But I wasn't. "Matt, I'm not a defender, I'm a scorer," I said. "The first time I played defense was last week. I'm lost back there."

"Back home, you're a scorer. Back home, pretty much everyone at this camp is a scorer. That's what happens when you're the best girl on your team. Your coach throws you up front and you dominate the other team all by yourself. Am I right?"

"Well, yeah, but—"

"If you've learned anything here it's that a national team is not a bunch of individuals. It's one group working together." He picked a soccer ball up off the floor and spun it like a basketball on his right index finger. "Trust me, you're a defender. An *attacking* defender, if that makes you feel any better." Matt waited for me to say something, but when I didn't, he said, "Do you know how many goals Brandi Chastain scored as a left back?"

I rolled my eyes and said, "Don't tell me, she was a forward who'd been converted to left back?"

"Spot on, mate."

I was speechless except for a tiny, whispered, "Oh."

Matt laughed. "With your excellent ball skills and touch you can win the ball, then make runs up the left flank and score goals with your awesome left peg . . . all from the left back position."

I heard Matt, but I didn't. I was still stuck on *left back*. "Is this because of my hamstring?" Matt flicked the ball with his left hand to keep it spinning, but didn't say anything. "Today's the last day of camp." *It's not fair.*

Matt popped the ball up and caught it with both hands. "Hard cheese."

"Wha—"

"Tough luck," he said. "Look on the bright side, you've got two games today to convince me you're U-15 material."

I hate you right now.

He held up both index fingers and then pointed them at me like guns. "Two games."

"May I go?"

Matt nodded.

I grabbed my bag. "Is this another one of your tests?" I couldn't believe those words had just come out of my mouth, but there was no stopping me. "Because I'm tired of taking tests."

Matt threw his head back and laughed. "See you on the pitch, kidda."

The minute I was outside again, I ripped off an e-mail to Coach Roy.

They've made me a LEFT BACK! On the LAST DAY OF CAMP. Can you believe it??

It's not like I expected Coach Roy to write back immediately, I just needed to get it off my chest. To tell someone who would understand. But when my phone vibrated a couple minutes later, I grabbed it out of my pocket and held my breath to see what Coach had to say about this ridiculous position change.

Left back? Interesting. Actually, I like it. Defense doesn't have to be boring. You've got the creativity and play-making skills to distribute the ball out of the back.

Not what you wanted to hear, huh? Relax. You're gonna be okay.

A couple of words of advice. Now that you're moving from the front line to the back line you need to adjust your mindset. A forward's job is to create; a defender's job is to destroy.

Keep your head in the game. Last day! DESTROY 'em!
Coach R

Chapter 42
Team 'Back

I didn't know what to think. And despite Coach Roy's e-mail I was still freaking out. The whole way to the field, I fought with myself. *Defense? Left back? And before the two most important games of camp?* I threw my boots at a chain link fence. Then I picked them up and threw them again. *Defense? Are you kidding me?* I looked up at the blue sky and yelled, "I hate your tests!"

I was early for training, so I stopped and waited for the others at the top of the hill above the soccer quilt. I was still grumbling when Nikesha and Sperry dropped their bags in front of me. "Well?" Nikesha asked.

I looked from Nikesha to Sperry and back again. "What?"

"Tell us what happened with Matt," Sperry demanded.

I kicked my boots. "I'm so mad I could—"

Nikesha stuck her index finger in my face and shook her braids from side to side. "No, he didn't cut you."

"He didn't cut me—"

"Duh," Sperry said. "Sorry, go on."

"He moved me to left back," I said. "Left. Back." I flopped down on the ground and lay spread-eagled. "On the last day of camp, with just two games to go, the two most important games of my life, with my entire future on the line, he makes me a defender. On the left flank. Where I have like zero experience."

Nikesha straddled me. She pinned my arms to the ground and shook her long braids in my face.

"Don't try to make me laugh," I said and pretended to pout. "I'm mad."

"Laugh, don't laugh, I don't care," Nikesha said and collapsed on the grass next to me. "This is so cool. You'll make a great 'back. I can't wait to play D with you today." She rolled over and slugged me in the arm. "Welcome to Team 'Back."

"Thanks, I guess."

Sperry knelt next to us, all elegant, not a hair out of place, everything tucked in. And to think I used to be intimidated by Sperry's perfect ways. Now I was proud to call her my friend. "You're a natural 'back," she agreed. "I don't know why we didn't think of this before."

"What do you mean?" I asked.

"You're tall, strong, confident, and you handle the ball like nobody's business." Sperry reached over and gently brushed a stray hair out of the corner of my mouth. "If I was on the other team, I'd hate to have to get past you to score."

"That's so nice," I said. "But I'm still mad at Matt."

"Fair enough." Nikesha picked a few blades of grass and threw them in the breeze. "But Flora, you have to look down the road. You have to think like a future national team player. Powerful, athletic girls like you are going to transform the international game."

I jumped on top of them, and the three of us formed a rolling hug as we tumbled down the grassy hill. We sat up laughing just as Tatiana and Kaylee strolled by.

"Oh, look," Tatiana said. "The loser's a lesbian."

"Tatiana," I said all patient and slow, like a teacher talking to a kindergartener. "I'm not Lebanese. I'm American."

Kaylee surprised me by busting out laughing. She shut up, though, when Tatiana shot her a look of death.

"Whatever," Tatiana said, grabbing Kaylee's arm and pulling her toward the bench.

Sperry smiled at me. "Good one, Maine-y," she said. "But you realize that joke flew over her head?"

"That's exactly why I said it."

"Let's go play some 'back," Nikesha said.

When we reached the benches, the coaches were huddled together. Something was up. *No more bad news*, I thought to myself.

"Wakey, wakey," Matt said as he climbed up on a bench. "Today's our last day, so we're going to make some changes to the teams."

Some of the girls groaned. Others held hands. We all knew what this meant. Another cut.

"We're going to name two teams of fifteen girls each. That's thirty girls, for you non-maths geniuses. The final two teams will play a game this morning and another late this afternoon. If we don't call your name, we need you to move over to the far fields and join Laura and Erika, where you'll be playing games as well."

Matt signaled for Rainey to join him on the bench. "You want to read off the list?" he asked her. "Since no one can understand a word I say." We all laughed nervously.

I realized I was holding my breath. I forced myself to exhale. I had to have made the cut. Matt wouldn't have put me through the whole "We're changing your position" thing for nothing. *Would he?* Rainey read off Team U first. The names, of course, weren't in alphabetical order. Each name she called was followed by a little yelp of joy. Kaylee and Tatiana made it. Ugh.

"Now here's Team S. Get it? Teams U & S? U.S.?" No one laughed.

"Just read the names," someone in the back said.

"All righty then." Rainey looked at her list. Math geniuses or not, we all knew there were only fifteen spots left for forty-five girls. I did the calculation in my head . . . just slightly more than a thirty-three percent chance of being named to Team S. . . . I didn't like those odds.

I counted down from fifteen in my head. I heard Rainey announce Nikesha's name. Zoe's. And then Sperry's. After Sperry there were six spots left. Five. Four. Three. I was going to strangle Matt. Two.

"And last, but not least, Flora Dupre."

Everybody stood up. Some girls hugged. Some screamed. Some slunk off toward the far fields. I sat stone-still. I wasn't sure if Rainey had actually said, "And last, but not least, Flora Dupre," or if I'd imagined the words in my head.

"Get up, girl," Nikesha said. "Team 'Back's got some work to do."

"I made it? Did I make it?" I felt like I was going to throw up.

"Earth to Flora. You're in." Sperry and Nikesha threw their arms around me. The way we jumped up and down you'd have thought we just defeated Germany for the Algarve Cup.

"We're in. We're in. We're in," we said together.

I turned to Nikesha. "Just so you know, I'm still mad at Matt."

"Whatever floats your boat. Just remember you're a 'back now. That's where the happenin' chicks hang."

"Yeah, yeah, Team 'Back, rah rah rah."

Nikesha tugged my shorts halfway down my backside before running onto the pitch.

"I'll get you, my pretty," I said. "And your little dog, too."

I pulled my pants back up to waist level. *You're a left back now*, I told myself. *Deal with it.* Then I reached up and touched Ma's soccer ball charm.

Follow my dream, no matter what, right, Ma?

Chapter 43
Discombobulated

From the opening whistle I was out of sorts. It felt so weird not being on the forward line—at the center of it all—in such an important game. Most of the time I played too far up, and Rainey had to remind me to stay back. And Matt, who was usually quite vocal, only said one thing to me in the first half, "Flora, engage brain."

When he said it, I wanted to scream at him, *I wouldn't have to if you'd kept me up front! I didn't have to think up there. I just played.* But then I caught myself. *You're a 'back now, deal with it. The coaches don't expect miracles.*

I was so thankful to have Nikesha with me on the back line. In the quieter moments—when our teammates had the ball in Team U's last third—Nikesha encouraged me and gave me tips. "Whatever you do," she said, "don't block the keeper's view of the ball. If she can't follow the action, you're creating a scoring opportunity."

"That's the opposite of how a forward thinks."

"Yup, but you're a 'back now—"

"I know, get with the program already," I said.

During a brief break in play, Rainey waved me over to the touchline. "As a defender," she said, "it's fine to make runs, but you've got to pick your moments. You don't want to run all the way up the field and then be too exhausted to get back into position on defense."

After play was underway again, Kaylee lofted a long ball into our final third. It was intended for Tatiana, but I used my body to shield her, got control of the ball, and started the attack with an outlet pass to Zoe. Two weeks ago, on that horrible bus ride from the airport to the ISA, I never, ever would have imagined myself a) standing up to a Queen B, or b) working with one to foil the other two. My, how things change.

Rainey yelled from the bench. "That's it, Flora! Way to use your body." I smiled at Rainey and thought to myself, *That's right, I'm big, I'm strong, and I don't let Queen Bs score on my watch.*

All thirty of us knew the coaches were looking to see who took what they learned in the last two weeks and was able to use it in pressure-cooker game situations. Matt had made it clear that if a girl thought and played like an individual, she wouldn't make the team.

"Flora," Meagan our goalkeeper called out. "Mark her."

I looked up and saw Tatiana, all tanned legs and blonde ponytail flying up the flank. *You are a mean person*, I thought to myself, *and I will not let you make me look bad*. I focused on Tatiana's feet but then remembered something Nikesha had said about playing defense—keep your eye on the ball not on the player. And I did. The next time I saw the ball shift to the right, I slid in feet first and knocked the ball out from under her. As I watched my teammates regain possession, run the ball up the field, and score, I realized Nikesha was right. If you watched the ball there was less chance the girl with the ball could fake you out with her body movements.

The coaches called us in for a water break. Rainey came up behind me and said, "That sequence started with you. Good job."

"So in a twisted way," I said, "defenders can start a goal-scoring run."

"There's nothing twisted about it. Defenders always start the attack. They don't just defend," Rainey said. "I'll take an attacking defender over a stationary defender any day."

"Like Cat Whitehill?"

"Exactly. When the pressure's on, Cat's right there defending the goal, but she's not afraid to be a playmaker and distribute the ball out of the back."

"Now that you mention it," I said, thinking, "it does seem like Cat's all over the field."

"She's an attacking defender," Rainey said. "That's what we want you to be. You've got the ball skills and touch to keep possession, then make runs up the left flank and score with either foot. All from the left back position."

"I guess I never thought of defenders as scorers."

"It's probably time you get your head around that." Rainey gently tugged my ponytail.

I stared toward the mountains and thought back to Matt's speech early on in camp. *Your assignment for the next two weeks is to play smart soccer.*

I wanted nothing more than to play smart soccer, but it, well, it kind of hurt, not to be playing up front. Even if Rainey said defenders can score, their main job is still defense—why else would they be called defenders?

Nikesha squirted me with her drink bottle. "What are you frowning about?"

"I'm just trying to make sense of playing in the back."

"What's to make sense of? The ball comes at you. You stop it from going in the goal. End of story."

"It's not that simple," I said. "You've always been a defender, right?"

Nikesha raised her hands and fluffed an imaginary, gargantuan Afro. "And a very good one I might add."

"It's hard for me. When you're a forward, you feel like a superstar—like the most important player on the field— because you score goals. If you don't put the ball in the net, you don't win."

Nikesha nodded her head. "Go on."

"It's embarrassing to admit, but I like the attention of playing up front. Playing defense, I feel a bit more like a worker bee." I knelt down to adjust the tongue of my boot. I looked up at Nikesha. "I know you've always been a defender, so don't take this the wrong way, but it feels like a demotion."

"You're right; defense isn't glamorous. But winning isn't just about scoring goals. It's also about stopping the other team from scoring," she said. "How do you think goalkeepers feel? They never get credit when their team wins, and it's always their fault when they lose."

Good point, I thought.

Nikesha took a long drink. "It's like Matt said, we can't think like individuals anymore, and we can't play like individuals. We need to act like a national team—not some dopey high school team, where Flora Dupre does everything by herself to win."

I ran my hands through my hair, re-did my ponytail, and nodded in agreement. But I was still trying to figure out how to be a defender and an attacker at the same time.

It was going to take some getting used to.

Chapter 44
Nutmegged

From the opening whistle of the second half, play was rough. All thirty of us wanted to be named to the U-15s tonight. None of us wanted to be on Matt's list of players that might make the team later in the year. No, we wanted to secure a spot. Today. But Matt had been so secretive that we didn't even know how many girls he was going to name tonight—we guessed it would be about a dozen or so.

As I fended off attack after attack by Team U, I thought about what Nikesha had said. She was right: playing defense was stressful, a different kind of stressful than playing up front, and not one I was used to. My biggest problem was that my teammates controlled the ball so well, it rarely left Team U's end, so I spent big chunks of time standing around watching. On any other day I would have been thrilled that we were dominating our opponents, but I only had today's two games to prove I was a U-15 caliber defender, and I couldn't do that if the ball stayed down at the other end of the pitch. It took everything I had not to scream at my teammates, *Come on you guys, stop hogging the ball!*

When Rainey announced there were fifteen minutes left in the second half, a wave of panic raced through my body. I rose up on my toes, danced around to stay sharp, and told myself, *Engage brain, engage brain*.

I watched as Sperry fired one past their keeper to put us up 3–0. Normally I would have run up field, jumped on her back, and congratulated her. Not now, not with less than fifteen minutes left. Instead, I jogged over, high-fived her, then returned to my spot on the left flank.

I reached inside my jersey and touched the soccer ball charm. *This is good*, I told myself. *The ball's back at the center stripe. Maybe Team U can get it into our end. Come on, you stupid Queen Bs, help me out here.*

Tatiana and Kaylee were on Team U's front line, standing opposite Zoe on our front line. If there weren't so much at stake, I might have found it funny. Shortly after the restart, Tatiana cut neatly around Sperry at midfield and drove the ball to Kaylee, who flew up the pitch toward me. I staked my ground. I knew Kaylee had terrific dribbling skills, so I reminded myself to watch the ball, not her body. When Kaylee reached me, we jostled for possession. I used my size and weight to lean into her. When that didn't work, I tried to nudge my foot between her legs, but every time, she kept the ball just barely out of my reach.

I imagined taking the ball off her and making a run up the flank. Then Kaylee leaned left, and I covered with a big step to the right. Too big. *Too big. Come back.* But it was too late. Kaylee plugged the ball between my legs, slipped around me, and reclaimed the ball. I couldn't believe it. She nutmegged me. That dirty rat nutmegged me.

With no one between her and the keeper, Kaylee calmly nailed a shot deep to the upper left corner of the net. Team U was on the board—they went nuts.

Rainey blew the whistle to mark the end of the game. I stood and stared at the ball in the back of the net. I'd spent most of the second half waiting for something to happen, and then when I had my chance to impress Matt, to be a true attacking defender, I let a Queen B nutmeg me.

After a minute or so, I forced myself to walk toward the benches, where both teams were grabbing their sweats and heading off to lunch. I caught Kaylee's eye and told myself to do like Mémère and kill her with kindness. "Awesome goal," I said. "And the nutmeg. Nice move, I'm just sorry it happened to me."

"Thanks." Kaylee blushed. "I wasn't trying to make you look bad. It just kind of happened."

"It was smooth," I said and walked toward the bench to gather my things.

Nikesha came up behind me. "Aren't you the gracious one?"

I batted my eyelashes and curtsied. "She's okay," I said. "I think Tatiana's the real problem."

Instinctively, Nikesha and I both looked over at Zoe, who was shoving stuff in her bag. Zoe looked up. "What?" she asked. "Do I have something in my teeth?"

I'd been feeling guilty about lumping Zoe into the Queen Bs. And now I realized I was probably wrong about Kaylee, too.

During rest period, Samantha and I lay on our beds with our legs raised against the wall. "You're not going to believe this,"

Samantha said. "But I'm seriously, seriously, seriously think-ing about moving to the Academy full-time."

"That's amazing." I felt a twinge of jealousy, but pushed it away.

"I know, right?" she said. "I mean, the national coaches have been bugging me for a long time to move here and train with them. And this morning after practice they said it would be a really good idea if I moved here soon, you know, with Pac Rims coming up and the Youth Olympic Games less than a year away."

"How would that work?"

"U.S. Gymnastics pays for everything. All I do is show up—"

"And train for like eight hours a day," I added.

"Oh yeah, there's that." Samantha laughed. "But seri-ously, I'm tired of always moving around because of my dad's job. Always changing gyms. I'm lucky now being at Bart and Nadia's gym because the coaching's good, but I'm the only international elite there, so there's no other girls to push me. I need that competition on a daily basis."

I nodded. *I need that, too*, I thought.

"Every time I come to one of these camps," Samantha said, "I realize how much faster I'd improve if I trained here every day. I look around and my routines aren't as clean as the other girls'. At the Elite level you have to work so hard to gain a tenth of a point in the judges' eyes." She hugged her knees to her chest.

I was happy for Samantha. I was. But it was a lot to take in, especially with the image of Kaylee passing the ball between my legs still on instant replay in my brain. "Do you think your parents will let you do it? Leave home?"

"I've been dropping hints for months. My mom seems cool about it, but you never know with the General. Part of me wants to move here so he can't keep an eye on my injuries. So I can stop running off to see doctors and concentrate on preparing for Pac Rims."

"So what's the plan?"

"I've got two more weeks of camp, then I'll go home and see what they say."

"It would be wicked cool to live here," I said.

"I know," Samantha agreed.

I had to get my mind in a better place, so I picked up my headphones. I swung my legs down, shifted my pillow back up to the headboard, crawled under the covers, and pressed play. For an hour, I lay motionless—not awake, but not asleep, either. I caught myself making little snoring noises as Charley's voice ran through my head.

I'd used Charley's hypnosis recording once so far, and I loved it. Like Samantha, I couldn't explain how it worked, but it did. It totally put me in the zone.

When the recording clicked off, I opened my eyes and stared at the ceiling. I remembered bits and pieces of what I'd listened to. Last night I didn't remember any of it. But today I woke up ready to play smart soccer. I thought about being strong and confident, about taking chances and looking for opportunities on the field. I thought about being an attacking defender. The morning game hadn't gone as I'd hoped, but the afternoon game was going to be a different story.

No one—not Tatiana, not Matt, not the entire Team U—could stand in my way. I was ready to show Matt I deserved to be on the U-15s. I owed it to my family. To Pépère. To myself.

Chapter 45
Own Goal

When I reached the top of the hill by the soccer quilt, I couldn't believe how many people had gathered to watch the final game of U-14 Girls' National Team ID Camp. You'd have thought we were playing an international. All seventy of the girls who had been cut earlier in camp were there. So were the entire camp coaching staff, a dozen or so U.S. Soccer officials, a handful of trainers and sports psychologists, and the head coach for the U.S. Women's National Team.

Normally this would have freaked me out, but I was ready to play in front of a crowd. I had something to prove. The more people who saw my skills, the better.

Both sides started out in a 4-3-3 formation, with four defenders, three midfielders, and three girls up front. I was at left back, Nikesha was next to me, Sperry was in front of us in the midfield, and Zoe was opposite Tatiana and Kaylee on the front line.

The first half got off to a fierce start. It was clean but tough soccer. Nikesha, Sperry, Zoe, and I played like a well-oiled unit. Nikesha and I used our small-group defending skills to take the ball off Tatiana and Kaylee. I used my body, Nikesha used her quick feet, and Sperry and Zoe waited on the edges to pick up the ball and run with it. Our teamwork resulted in two first-half goals, one for Sperry and one when I dribbled up three-quarters of the field and crossed it to Zoe for a header.

I felt the most comfortable I'd ever felt on defense and was proud of my play. Nikesha and I kept a running dialogue going throughout the game. The only unsettling thing was that for the first time since camp began, the coaches were completely silent. I glanced at Matt several times and wished I could tell what he was thinking. Every so often the Women's National Team coach leaned in to say something, and Matt nodded in agreement. I willed them to please be talking about me. To name me to the U-15s.

During a stoppage in play, while Tatiana lay sprawled on the pitch clutching her left knee—couldn't have happened to a nicer girl—I reached up and touched the soccer ball charm. I watched the trainers load Tatiana onto a stretcher. Part of me wished I felt bad for her, even just a little bit, but all I heard in my head was Mémère's voice saying, "What goes around comes around." The golf cart zipped past me and I thought to myself, *It's official. Your nasty behavior has come back and bitten you in the knee. Buh-bye.*

Sperry joined me at the touchline. "Karma," she said.

"I know." I offered Sperry a sip from my bottle. "I'm as competitive as the next girl," I said. "But honestly, I think you can be a nice person and still be super-competitive."

Sperry raised her fist in the air. "Right on, sistuh," she said, and we both laughed.

Play started back up and we continued to dominate Team U.

At one point, Sperry took a direct kick that resulted in a Beckham-esque goal into the upper left corner of the net. Off the restart, Team U's Hanna dumped it off to Kaylee, who did a step over and pushed the ball past Zoe and continued to weave her way through my teammates. She was headed right for the goal when I stopped her and sent it forward to one of my teammates.

Brain. Officially. Engaged.

I stole a glance at Matt. Nothing.

With time running out and the first half almost over, Team U tried again to break through our defense. When Kaylee neared the 18, she fired a rocket off her right foot. Nikesha stepped into the path of the ball. It hit her thigh and ricocheted behind her, just to the right of the near post.

With only Tatiana's injury time left on the clock, Team U hustled to get in a final corner. I posted up on their tallest girl, Hanna. The ball lofted toward the far post. Hanna and I jumped in unison. Both of us stretched our necks to reach the ball. My extra four inches helped me get to it first. I threw my head around to clear the ball to the left.

No. No.

I cleared the ball, but in the wrong direction. I'd aimed for an open area just up field. Instead the ball flew off my forehead and into the goal. *My goal.* Past *my* goalie.

An own goal.

In all my years playing soccer, I'd never scored an own goal. The whistle blew. The first half was over. Once again, I stood frozen to the pitch. I turned to our keeper, Meagan. "I'm so sorry."

"Honest mistake," she said. "We've got another half to play."

I scanned the sidelines for Matt—*tell me you didn't see*

that—but I couldn't find him. I walked toward the benches and then I saw him, deep in conversation with the Women's National Team coach. I had to walk by them to get to the drink bottles. I took a deep breath. They were having an animated conversation. I could have sworn I heard Matt say *oh-gee*, his word for an own goal. The moment I got up next to them, they stopped talking, looked at me, watched me walk past, and then returned to their conversation.

Please tell me you're not talking about me.

I felt like everyone was watching me. I'd scored an own goal in the most important game of camp. What's the expression: people only remember the last five minutes of something? Lucky oh-gee me.

I sipped from my drink bottle, wanting to cry, and reminded myself of something Coach Roy liked to say. *Never let the other team know what you're thinking. Keep the same expression on your face, whether you're happy, sad, or frustrated.*

And so I did. I stretched with Sperry and kept my game face on, even though inside I was falling apart. I'd given Matt a very real reason to leave me off the team. I couldn't help but think this never would have happened if he'd have left me on the forward line.

Sperry raised an eyebrow as we sat on the ground stretching each other's legs. "You okay?"

"Yeah, yeah. I'm fine." I gently pulled Sperry's arms toward me. "The game's only half over."

"Good girl," she said.

I may have messed up my chances of making the U-15s, but I wasn't going down without a fight.

⚽   ⚽   ⚽

As I jogged onto the pitch for the final forty-five minutes of ID Camp, I noticed Logan and his buddies standing behind our goal. When we made eye contact, Logan pumped his fist and gave me a smile that said, *You can do it!*

And I knew I could, but I spent the entire second half chasing opportunities just to touch the ball. Every time Team U tried to advance the ball, our midfielders stopped them and returned it back to Team U's final third. All I wanted to do was play an attacking role, but the ball never seemed to cross the midfield. It felt like the soccer gods were against me. *Why did I have to be on such a good team?*

We quickly ran the score up to 6–1. With every passing minute, I became more and more panicky inside. My national team dream was slipping away, and there was nothing I could do to stop it. Nikesha saw action a couple of times when Kaylee brought the ball up the right flank, but I spent the second half on the periphery of the action.

When the final whistle blew—the final whistle of ID Camp—I knew my dream was over. I felt myself start to hyper-ventilate. My breath got more and more shallow. *Do not do this*, I told myself. *Do not let them know what you're think-ing.* I concentrated as hard as I possibly could to get my breath under control. I walked to the sidelines and made a point of slapping hands with every girl—okay, every girl except Tatiana, who was back from the trainer's room and sporting a set of crutches—and every ID Camp coach. When I got to Matt, I said, "Thank you for everything. This was the opportunity of a lifetime."

The opportunity of a lifetime I threw away with an own goal.

Despite the anger and disappointment, I kept a smile

plastered on my face. I even joked around with Zoe and Hanna as we walked back to the dorms. I listened to their excited chatter, but all I could think about was getting back to Beijing so I could cry. Matt was going to announce his U-15 Girls' National Team selections after dinner. I had to get this out of my system if I wanted to pull myself together by then. My dream was over, I knew that, but I had to find some way to be happy for Nikesha and Sperry when they made the team. Because they *would* make the team. And they deserved it.

I looked down at my phone—six new e-mails. I couldn't read them, not now. I shoved the phone back in my pocket. What was I going to tell everyone back home? *I suck, end of story.*

End of dream.

Chapter 46
Without Freddy Adu

After bawling in the shower for a half hour, I felt a little better. At least I knew I wouldn't cry when I *officially* found out that I hadn't made the U-15s. And that was only because there wouldn't be any tears left. I still couldn't face the e-mails from home, which had doubled to a dozen while I was in the shower.

On my way to the dining hall, I ran into Sally and Charley at the front desk. "I heard you played well today," Sally said. "Good on you."

Me? I played well? "Thanks, Sally. I—I tried my best."

"You showed great maturity and poise out there," Charley said. "I'm proud of you."

I didn't know what to say. In my heart, I truly believed I played poorly. But Charley was there. She saw the game. Maybe I'd played well enough to make the U-15s, but I'd scored an own goal and I'd barely touched the ball in the second half. I didn't know what to believe. "They're all great players," I said. "It's anyone's guess what Matt will decide."

"Well, I was impressed with how you handled the own goal," Charley said.

"It was a mistake. What could I do?"

"You could have let it get you down," she said. "You could have cried. You could have freaked out."

"Yeah, well, I decided to freak out about it later," I said. "I even pictured where I'd do it. In the shower."

Charley smiled. "That's wonderful, Flora. Do you mind if I suggest that to some of the other athletes I work with?"

"What, that they cry in the shower? I don't think it's a novel idea."

"No, how you consciously decided to deal with the disappointment and anger later," she said.

"Matt told me there's no crying in soccer."

"Oh, that Matt," Charley said. "He's a sensitive creature, isn't he?"

"Do I have to answer?" We all laughed.

"Your family would be so proud of you, Flora," Sally said.

I touched the charm, which was back on its chain.

"Good luck tonight," Charley said. "You deserve the world, young lady."

An hour later, when I slipped in through the back doors, the auditorium was packed with nervous teenage girls. I tried to be invisible in the bustling auditorium. I chose a spot near the back, among a group of girls that were cut the first week of camp, and slunk down low in a seat. Then I had second thoughts. Maybe it was bad luck to sit next to them—they definitely weren't going to make the team. I stood up and walked toward the middle of the room, where Nikesha saw me and waved. "We saved you a seat," she said.

I slowly made my way toward Nikesha. When I realized she and Sperry were sitting with Zoe and Kaylee, I smiled for the first time since the game. Poor Tatiana lost her sidekicks!

I sat down between Sperry and Nikesha, plastered a smile on my face, and tried not to think about my oh-gee in the first half or barely touching the ball in the second half. "This is so exciting," I said.

Zoe leaned over, giggled, and said, "Gee, ya think?" And we all laughed.

Matt climbed onto the stage and the house lights dimmed. The wall behind him came to life with the words: U.S. SOCCER UNDER-14 GIRLS' NATIONAL DEVELOPMENT IDENTIFICATION CAMP. The whole auditorium, including me, jumped out of our seats and hooted and hollered. After a few moments, Matt motioned for us to sit back down.

He looked out over the audience and said, "Every single one of you girls should be proud of yourself. It's been an incredible two weeks. If you girls are the future of U.S. women's football, the rest of the world should be shaking in their boots."

The room erupted again.

"You made it very difficult for me," he said. "But before I name the girls who have been selected for the U-15s, let me just say that if your name is not called, it's not the end of the world. Far from it. It simply means that right now, today, you're not ready to play for a national team."

I looked around the room and tried to take in the moment. It had been an amazing two weeks. Tomorrow morning I had to leave all of this behind to go home. It was weird to think about going home. I missed everyone, especially Pépère, but leaving here was going to be hard. How could Acadia ever compare to the International Sports Academy? I pushed the thought out of my head and tried to concentrate on what Matt was saying.

"I want to talk about one more thing before I name the team," Matt said. "This camp was about determining attitude and potential. You are all excellent soccer players, but it takes more than soccer skills to play for a U.S. National Team. You need to have the right attitude. You need to be a team player. You need to treat your teammates with respect. Some of you fell short on this. Very short. We will not tolerate bullies and divisive young ladies in U.S. Soccer."

I noticed several girls turn around and look at Tatiana. *Good*, I thought, *so the coaches were aware of her attitude after all.*

Matt stepped to the side and pointed to the wall behind him. "Right then. Are you ready?" he asked. The projection changed to read: U.S. SOCCER UNDER-15 GIRLS' NATIONAL TEAM.

We jumped to our feet again. Tatiana started to chant U-S-A. U-S-A. I nudged Sperry and said, "Tatiana had no idea Matt was talking about her, did she?" And we both rolled our eyes.

Matt waved his arms and everyone slowly settled back into their seats. "By the end of the year," he said, "I'm going to pick twenty-five girls for the U-15s. I've chosen ten of you from this camp. That means there are still fifteen spots up for grabs between now and December. I'd like the girls I call to come up onto the stage with me. So, without Freddy Adu, I mean further ado . . . little U.S. Soccer humor for you . . . Any chance? . . . No."

Each name Matt announced appeared on the wall behind him. Nikesha was the second girl chosen. Sperry and I hugged her before she ran up to the stage.

Eight to go. Eight to go. *Come On.*

Kaylee.

Seven more. *Come on you wackadoodle. Call me.*

I agreed with each pick. They were all team players and they all had phenomenal talent. Sperry and I held hands so tightly our knuckles turned white. I felt her grip release when Matt called her name. I was happy for her. Truly happy.

Two more. Two more.

The last thing I heard Matt say was, "May I present the U-15s."

He hadn't called my name. Zoe looked at me briefly—she had tears in her eyes. Then she got up and walked away quickly.

I wanted to sprint from the auditorium, but I was frozen in my chair. *Run, run,* I told myself. The other girls started to stream out into the hallway, and still I couldn't make my body move. *Do not cry. Do not cry,* I implored.

I watched Sperry and Nikesha jump off the stage and dash out the side doors. I knew they were looking for me, but I stayed locked in my chair. I wanted to call to them, but no sound came out when I opened my mouth.

Now that I'd had a taste of what it was like to live and train as an elite athlete, how could I go back to Acadia? I wanted to stay at the Academy. I wanted to be on the U-15s.

The lights on the stage snapped off. The words on the back wall disappeared, and the house lights came up. I sat by myself in the glaring light.

I couldn't believe it. I'd tried so hard to play my best, to be a team player. But I'd failed. Here I was, still an individual. Alone.

Chapter 47
Not the End of the World

"Mind if I join you?" Matt stood in the row in front of me.

I shook my head no, although I meant *Yes!* Matt sat in the seat in front of me and turned his body sideways to look at me.

"I can imagine how disappointed you are," he said, and then waited for my response. When I didn't say anything he continued. "Flora, I was impressed with you on so many levels these past two weeks."

I gave him a puzzled look. "You were?"

"You showed incredible maturity. You worked hard. You were kind to the other girls. You showed the coaches respect. And let's face it, you were put through the ringer by Tatiana—"

"You noticed?"

"Who didn't?" he said. "I'm sorry you had to put up with that crap."

Wow. Who was this warm and fuzzy Matt? "I thought you didn't like me," I said.

"Flora, it's not about liking or not liking you. I have to

keep my distance; that's how I coach. I need to stand back, to figure out which combination of players forms the best team. What you showed me is that you're a team player. You could be one of the best attacking defenders to ever play the women's game. You and Nikesha, you're the future of U.S. defense."

"So why didn't you name me to the U-15s?"

"You need more experience. You need to play more. You need better conditioning and training—"

"I know, I know," I said. "When I get back to Maine, I'm going to stop playing other sports and completely focus on soccer."

"That's what I want to talk to you about," he said. "We'd like to have you live in residence for a year at the Academy."

"Wait. What?" I was speechless. "I can't afford—"

"You're part of U.S. Soccer now," he said. "We'll pay for it. We believe in your talent."

"But—"

"The Women's National Team head coach liked what she saw out there."

"Even my own goal?"

"Especially the oh-gee. She said you handled that better than most of her national team girls would have." Matt took a moment for his words to sink in. "Did you know Brandi Chastain scored an oh-gee in the '99 World Cup?"

"Really?" I said.

"Yeah, it was against Germany in the quarters. She scored an oh-gee early in the first half, but in the forty-ninth minute she came back and scored a goal—a real goal—off a corner kick. Tied the game up. The U.S. went on to win 3–2. And the rest, you know, is history," Matt said.

"I get it, an oh-gee at ID Camp's not the end of the world."

"You're always going to make mistakes, that's football. What matters is how you handle those mistakes. I couldn't be more proud of you than if you were my own daughter." Matt reached into a bag at his feet. "Flora, you're the future of U.S. Women's Soccer, and we're going to do everything we can to support you." He handed me an International Sports Academy warm-up jacket. "Do you know what this is?"

"Yeah. The only kids who get them are full-time residents of the Academy." I unzipped the jacket and looked at him. He nodded, and I slipped it on.

"Welcome to the big time, kidda," he said. "Living at the Academy is going to do wonders for your game."

"And there's still a chance I can make the U-15s?"

"That's the plan. You just need to play more. That's how you'll develop. You can't do that in Maine."

"But my father—"

"I've already talked to him," Matt said.

"You have?" I could only imagine that conversation: silence meets silence.

"Yup. Our thought was that you could fly home tomorrow, spend a couple of weeks in Maine getting everything in order, and then come back to live here full-time. But, you need to decide if you can leave Maine."

"I'll never leave Maine, not forever," I said. "It's who I am. But I'm also a soccer, well, football player, and this is where I need to be. Maine isn't going anywhere. As long as I know my family is behind me, I'll be fine."

We walked to Matt's office so I could call Pa. By the time Matt unlocked the office door, I'd made up my mind. I was staying. But I also knew, despite Pa's recent encouraging e-mails, that he was against my coming to the Academy in the first place. And I was still only fourteen years old, and Pa was Pa. This was up to him.

I touched the soccer ball charm. *Ma*, I said, *I need a miracle here.*

Chapter 48
Resident

Ever since Ma died, I never knew which Pa would wake up in the morning—the fun, supportive one, or the sad, absent one. My stomach churned when I punched in the phone number for the farmhouse. I wasn't sure what I'd say to him. And worse, I had no idea what Matt had said to him.

"*Allô*, Pa?"

"Flora, *ma chérie! Je suis tellement content d'entendre ta voix.*" Whatever Matt had said, it worked. Pa had been waiting for my call.

"How's Pépère?" I asked.

"Doctor de la Chapelle says he'll be home soon. Gonna be good as new," he said. "But more importantly, how's my girl doing? I hear great things from your coach. He sounds like quite a fella, that Matt."

I laughed. "That's one way to describe him."

"Flora, I'm . . . well . . . we're all so proud of you. Your Ma, she'd—" Pa choked up.

"*Oui*—" I said. Pa and I didn't need to go there. We

knew what the other was thinking.

He cleared his throat. "I talked it over with Mémère and she agrees, you've got to follow your dream. We love you, and we're just a plane flight away."

"Oh, Pa, really?"

"We'd be crazy to stand in the way. But there's one thing I need to know—"

"I'll be safe here, Pa—"

"Ayuh, Matt guaranteed me of that," he said. "What I need to know is, is this what you want—"

"*Oui*—"

"Let me finish," he said. "I need to know *why* you want to do this."

"Because I love soccer."

"I realize that, but I don't want you to pursue soccer because it was your mother's dream. You're old enough to do what you want. Ma's gone. This is about you, Flora. We're talking about a big commitment, something you could end up doing for the rest of your life." He paused. I could hear him breathing. "I just need to know you're doing it for you, not for Ma."

I closed my eyes. I wasn't sure how to respond. I'd never actually thought of it that way. After a few moments I said, "I guess I play soccer because Ma loved it. But I love soccer because . . . because it's in my blood. Other than you and Mémère and Pépère and the farm, it's really the only thing I care about. It's kinda cool that Ma loved soccer, but this is different. This isn't dreaming about Soccerland, this is playing for the U.S.A. This is real. This is about becoming the best at something I love."

"What if I said you couldn't stay at the Academy?"

"Oh, Pa." I thought of Samantha's dad, who might make her quit gymnastics. "I'd die of a broken heart."

"Then it's settled," he said. "It's your passion, and it's your dream. We love you, Flora, and we support you."

I couldn't believe this was happening. "*Merci*, Pa. I love you, too."

"But Pa," I said, suddenly feeling guilty. "What about the farm?"

"Farm, shmarm!" We both laughed at Pa quoting Pépère. "So this Matt fella, he says you've got talent."

"Ayuh."

"Did it take him the whole two weeks to figure that one out?" Pa said.

"Looks that way."

"Maybe he's not as smart as I thought."

Oh, he's smart all right, I thought to myself. *He just needs a personality transplant.* "He's a wackadoodle, Pa."

"Got someone here who wants to talk to you. Hold on."

I knew immediately who it was. Rémi. "So," I asked him. "Do you forgive me?"

"Piss off, cuz," he said, and we both laughed.

When I hung up the phone, I went outside and found Matt sitting on my crying bench. He stood up and jammed his hands in his back pockets. "How'd it go?"

"He said I could stay." I threw my arms around Matt. The moment I did it, I knew I'd made a colossal mistake. Matt went stiff as a board, and I awkwardly untangled myself. "S-s-sorry," I said.

"That's all right," he laughed. "Just don't do it again—"

"I know, I know," I said. "No hugs or warm fuzzies. . . .

What did you say to my dad, anyway? It's like he did a complete one-eighty."

"I just spoke to him dad-to-dad," Matt said, blushing a little. "Now off you go. We'll talk tomorrow and get you set up as a resident. Congratulations, Flora."

"*Merci beaucoup*," I said and ran down the path.

It wasn't until I went to open the main Academy doors that I realized I'd spoken to Matt in French.

I shrugged my shoulders and thought, *Ayuh, if it's important, us Dupres say it in French*.

As I ran along the hallway toward Beijing, I glanced down at my new warm-up jacket. *Resident.* I liked the sound of that. I couldn't wait to share my good news. I had to find Nikesha and Sperry. Samantha. Logan.

I sprinted around the corner by the trainers' room and nearly cleaned out Tatiana. Before she could say anything I shouted, "Dump truck coming through!"

"Hey," Tatiana pointed at my warm-up jacket. "How'd you get that?" She shook her head so hard her ponytail swung around and pieces of it stuck to her lip gloss. "You can't wear that unless you're a resident athlete."

"The operative word in that sentence, Tatiana, is . . . resident," I said and took off running again. When I pushed open the doors to Beijing, I almost smacked into Zoe. We were both speechless. She had on an ISA warm-up jacket, too. "Are you?" she asked.

I nodded. "You?"

"Yes!" We both screamed and jumped into each others' arms. "Maybe we could room together," she said.

"I'd like that," I said. And I meant it. "I'll see you in two weeks."

"Deal, Roomie," she said, and we took off running in opposite directions.

I couldn't believe it. Tomorrow I was flying home to Maine. To Pa. To Mémère. To Pépère. To everyone who loved me. And in two weeks I was coming back to the International Sports Academy. To live. To train. To play for U.S. Soccer.

My dream was finally coming true.

Ma was right. There *was* a Soccerland. A real one. And now it was all mine.